MALGUDI ADVENTURES

Classic Tales for Children

R.K. Narayan

PUFFIN BOOKS

PUFFIN BOOKS
Published by the Penguin Group
Penguin Books India Pvt. Ltd, 7th Floor, Infinity Tower C, DLF Cyber City,
Gurgaon 122 002, Haryana, India
Penguin Group (USA) Inc., 375 Hudson Street, New York, New York 10014, USA
Penguin Group (Canada), 90 Eglinton Avenue East, Suite 700, Toronto, Ontario,
M4P 2Y3, Canada
Penguin Books Ltd, 80 Strand, London WC2R 0RL, England
Penguin Ireland, 25 St Stephen's Green, Dublin 2, Ireland (a division of Penguin
Books Ltd)
Penguin Group (Australia), 707 Collins Street, Melbourne, Victoria 3008, Australia
Penguin Group (NZ), 67 Apollo Drive, Rosedale, Auckland 0632, New Zealand
Penguin Books (South Africa) (Pty) Ltd, Block D, Rosebank Office Park, 181 Jan
Smuts Avenue, Parktown North, Johannesburg 2193, South Africa

Penguin Books Ltd, Registered Offices: 80 Strand, London WC2R 0RL, England

First published in Puffin by Penguin Books India 2004

Copyright © The Legal Heirs of R.K. Narayan 2004

32 31 30 29 28

Reprinted in 2014

ISBN 9780143335900

For sale in the Indian Subcontinent and Singapore only

Typeset in Gill Sans by SÜRYA, New Delhi
Printed at Repro India Ltd., Navi Mumbai

A PENGUIN RANDOM HOUSE COMPANY

CONTENTS

PUBLISHER'S NOTE

Malgudi Adventures comprises twelve pieces. Nine of these are excerpts from R.K. Narayan's novels *The Financial Expert*, *The Man-eater of Malgudi*, *Mr Sampath*, *The Dark Room*, *The English Teacher*, *A Tiger for Malgudi*, *The Guide*, *The World of Nagaraj* and *The Bachelor of Arts*. The other three are short stories, previously published under the titles 'Uncle', 'Naga' and 'Nitya'. The pieces have been retitled and edited for inclusion in this volume with the consent of the legal heirs of R.K. Narayan.

MARGAYYA AND BALU

[Margayya, in the novel The Financial Expert, *sits under a banyan tree with his account book, and doles out financial advice to the denizens of Malgudi. The following passage is a humorous account of his now-affectionate, now-exasperated relationship with his young son Balu.]*

MARGAYYA DEPOSITED THE box under a bench in the front room of his house. His little son immediately came running out from the kitchen with a shout: 'Appa!—' and gripped his hand, asking: 'What have you brought today?' Margayya hoisted him up on his shoulder: 'Well, tomorrow I will buy you a new engine, a small engine.' The child was pleased to hear it. He asked, 'How small will the engine be? Will it be so tiny?' He indicated with his thumb and first finger a minute size. 'All right,' said Margayya and put him down.

This was almost a daily ritual. The boy revelled in visions of miniature articles—a tiny engine, tiny cows, a tiny table, tiny everything, of the maximum size of a mustard seed. Margayya put him down and briskly removed his upper cloth and shirt, picked up a towel that was hanging from a nail on the wall, and moved to the backyard. Beyond a small clump of banana trees, which waved their huge fan-like leaves in the darkness, there was a single well of crumbling masonry, with a pulley over its crossbar. Margayya paused for a moment to admire the starry sky. Down below at his feet the earth was damp and marshy. All the drain water of two houses flowed into the banana beds. It was a common backyard for his house and the one next door, which was his brother's. It was really a single house, but a partition wall divided it into two from the street to the backyard.

No. 14D, Vinayak Street had been a famous landmark, for it was the earliest house to be built in that area. Margayya's father was considered a hero for settling there in a lonely place where there was supposed to be no security for life or property. Moreover it was built on the fringe of a cremation ground, and often the glow of a burning pyre lit up its walls. After the death of the old man the brothers fell out, their wives fell out, and their children fell out. They could not tolerate the idea of even breathing the same air or being enclosed by the same walls. They got involved in litigation and partitioned everything that their father had left. Everything that could be cut in two with an axe or scissors or a knife was divided between them, and the other things were catalogued, numbered and then shared out. But one thing that could neither be numbered nor cut up was the backyard of the house with its single well. They could do nothing about it. It fell to Margayya's share, and he would willingly have seen his brother's family perish without water by closing it to them, but public opinion prevented the exercise of his right. People insisted that the well should remain common property, and so the dividing wall came up to it, and stopped there, the well acting as a blockade between the two brothers, but accessible from either side.

Now Margayya looked about for the small brass pot. He could not see it anywhere.

'Hey, little man!' he called out, 'where is the well pot?' He liked to call his son constantly. When he came home, he could not bear to be away from him even for a moment. He felt uneasy and irritated when the child did not answer his call. He saw the youngster stooping over the lamp, trying to thrust a piece of paper into the chimney. He watched him from the doorway. He suppressed the inclination to call him away and warn him. The child thrust a piece of paper into the lamp, and when it burned brightly he recoiled at the sudden spurt of fire. But when it blackened and burnt out he drew near the lamp again gingerly putting his finger near the metal plate on the top. Before Margayya could stop him, he had touched it. He let out a shriek. Margayya was beside him in a moment. His shriek brought in Margayya's wife, who had gone to a neighbouring shop. She came rushing into the house with cries of 'What is it? What is it? What has happened?' Margayya felt embarrassed, like a man caught shirking a duty. He told his wife curtly, 'Why do you shout so much, as if a great calamity had befallen this household—so that your sister-in-law in the neighbourhood may think how active we are, I suppose!'

'Sister-in-law—how proud you are of your relatives!' Her further remarks could not be continued because of the howling set up by the child, whose burnt finger still remained unattended. At this the mother snatched him up from her husband's arms, and hugged him close to her, hurting him more, whereupon he shouted in a new key. Margayya tried to tear him out of his wife's arms, crying: 'Quick, get that ointment. Where is it? You can keep nothing in its place.'

'You need not shout!' the wife answered, running about and rummaging in the cupboard. She grumbled: 'You can't look after him even for a second without letting him hurt himself.'

4

'You need not get hysterical about it, gentle lady, I had gone for a moment to the well.'

'Everyone gets tap-water in this town. We alone—' she began, attacking on a new front.

'All right, all right,' he said, curbing her, and turning his attention to the finger. 'You must never, never go near fire again, do you understand?'

'Will you buy me a little elephant tomorrow?' the child asked, his cheeks still wet with tears. By now they had discovered a little wooden crucible containing some black ointment in the cupboard, hidden behind a small basket containing loose cotton (which Margayya's wife twisted into wicks for the lamp in god's niche). She applied the ointment to the injured finger and set the child roaring in a higher key. This time he said, 'I want a big peppermint.'

At night when the lights were put out and the sounds of Vinayak Street had quietened, Margayya said to his wife, lying on the other side of their sleeping child: 'Do you know—poor boy! I could have prevented Balu from hurting himself. I just stood there and watched. I wanted to see what he would do alone by himself.' His wife made a noise of deprecation: 'It is as I suspected. You were at the bottom of the whole trouble. I don't know . . . I don't know . . . that boy is terribly mischievous . . . and you are . . . you are . . .' She could not find the right word for it. Her instinct

5

was full of foreboding, and she left the sentence unfinished. After a long pause she added: 'It's impossible to manage him during the afternoons. He constantly runs out of the house into the street. I don't have a moment's peace or rest.'

'Don't get cantankerous about such a small child,' said Margayya, who disliked all these adverse remarks about his son. It seemed to him such a pity that that small bundle of man curled beside him like a tiny pillow should be so talked about. His wife retorted: 'Yes, I wish you could stay at home and look after him instead of coming in the evening and dandling him for a moment after he has exhausted all his tricks.'

'Yes, gladly, provided you agree to go out and arrange loans for idiots.'

*

Margayya was sitting before his small box, examining the accounts written in his red book. His son came up to sit on his lap. Margayya said: 'Go and play, don't disturb me now,' and tried to keep him off. 'This is my play, I won't go,' said the child, pushing towards him again and climbing resolutely on his lap. Margayya had to peep over his head in order to look at the register before him; Balu's hair constantly tickled his nostrils and he felt irritated. He cried: 'Balu, won't you leave me alone? I will buy you a nice—'

'What?' asked the child.

'A nice little elephant.'

'All right, buy it now, come on.'

'No, no, not now ... I'm working now,' he said, pointing at the small register. Balu shot out his little leg and kicked away the register petulantly, and in the process the inkwell upset beside it and emptied on the page. Then the child stamped his heel on the ink and it splashed over Margayya's face and spoiled the entire book. Margayya felt maddened at the sight of it. He simply gripped the boy by his shoulder, lifted him as he would lift an unwanted cat, and almost flung him into a corner. Needless to say it made the child cry so loudly that his mother came running out of the kitchen, her eyes streaming with tears owing to the smoke there. 'What has happened? What has happened?' she cried, rushing towards the child, who, undaunted, was again making a dash for his father as he stooped over the wreckage trying to retrieve his damaged account book. 'Look what he has done,' he cried excitedly. 'This monkey!'

'*You* are a monkey!' cried the boy, hugging his father's knee as he was blotting the spilled ink.

'If you don't leave me, I'll—I'll—' he was too angry. 'I'll give you over to the temple priest ... He'll flay your skin.'

'He will give me plantains,' corrected the boy. He turned aside and suddenly pounced on the book, grabbed it and dashed off. His father ran after him with war cries. The boy dodged him here and there, going into this corner and darting into that. His tears had by now dried, he was enjoying the chase, and with hysterical laughter he was running hither and thither clutching the precious red note-book in his hand. It was a small space within which he ran, but somehow Margayya was unable to seize him. Margayya panted with the effort. He cried: 'If you don't stop, I'll flay you.'

'What is the matter with you? What has come over you?' asked the wife.

'I'm all right,' Margayya replied proudly. 'You'll see what I'll do to that little monkey, that devil you have begotten.' His wife gave some appropriate reply, and tried to help in the chase. She pretended to look away and suddenly darted across to seize the boy. But he was too swift even for her calculations. She only collided against her husband, which irritated him more; and it allowed the child to dash into the street with his prize, with his father at his heels. He cried impatiently to his wife, 'Get out of the way—you—' at which she turned and went back to the kitchen murmuring: 'What do I care? I only let the rice overboil watching this tomfoolery.' The boy dashed down the front steps,

8

with his father following him. Margayya was blind to all his surroundings—all he could see was the little boy with his curly hair, and the small red-bound book which was in his hand. Some passers-by in Vinayak Mudali Street stopped to watch the scene. Margayya cried shamelessly: 'Hold him! Hold him!' At which they tried to encircle the boy. It was evident that by now he had become completely intoxicated with the chase. Presently he found that he was being outnumbered and cornered. As a circle of hunters hemmed in, he did an entirely unexpected thing—he turned back as if coming into his father's arms, and as he was just about to grasp him, darted sideways to the edge of the gutter and flung the red book into it. The gutter ran in front of the houses; roaring waters went down the drain, God knew where. It was well known that any object which fell into it was lost for ever, it sank and went out of sight, sank deeper and deeper into a black mass, and was hopelessly gone. The gutter was wide as a channel. Once in a while, especially before the elections, the municipal officials came down and walked along the edge, peering into its dark current and saying something among themselves as to its being a problem and so on. But there they left it until the next election. It was a stock cynicism for people to say when they saw anyone inspecting the drains: 'They are only looking for the election votes there!' At other times the gutter continued its existence unhampered, providing the cloud of mosquitoes and the stench that characterized existence in Vinayak Mudali Street.

Presently a big crowd stood on the edge of the drain looking at its inky, swirling waters. People sympathized with Margayya. Wild, inaccurate reports of what had fallen into it were circulated. Margayya heard people tell each other: 'A box was dropped into it.' 'That child threw away a gold chain into it.'

Everyone looked at Balu with interest. He seemed to have become a hero for the moment. He felt abashed at this prominence and hung his head. The sun was shining on them fiercely, though it was just nine-thirty in the morning. Margayya looked red with anger and exertion. His son's face was also flushed. The little boy crossed his arms behind him and stood on the edge of the gutter, watching it with fascination. There was no trace of the book left anywhere. Margayya's blood boiled as he watched the unconcern of the boy, who, true to the type in that street, wore only a shirt covering the upper-half of his body. Two pedlars carrying green vegetables, a cyclist who jumped off on seeing the crowd, a few schoolchildren, a curd seller, and a few others formed the group which now watched the gutter, with varying comments passing between them. A man was saying: 'Some people are so fond that they give their children everything they ask for.' On hearing this Margayya felt so enraged that he lifted the edge of the shirt the little boy was wearing and slapped him fiercely across his uncovered seat. The boy cried aloud: 'Oh!' and turned round on his father. It started a fresh scene. Someone dragged away the child, saying: 'Save the child from this ruffian.' Another said: 'He would have pushed the child into the gutter.' A woman with a basket came forward to ask: 'Are you a heartless demon? How can you beat such a small child?' She flung down her basket and picked up the child on her arm. Balu copiously sobbed on her shoulder. Another woman tried to take him from her, commenting: 'Only those who bear the child for ten months in the womb know how precious it is. Men are always like this.' Someone objected to this statement; it turned out to be the man holding the cycle, who retorted with great warmth: 'Boys must be chastized; otherwise do you want them to grow up into devils?' Margayya looked at him gratefully. Here at last was a friend in this absolutely hostile world. He swept his arms to address all the women and the gathering: 'It's all very well for you to talk . . . But he has thrown in there an important account book. What am I to do without it?'

'How can a baby know anything about account books and such things? God gives children to those who don't deserve them.'

'You should not have kept it within his reach. You must always be prepared for such things where there are children.'

A washerwoman, who had come forward, said: 'You were childless for twelve years, and prayed to all the gods and went to Tirupati: was it only for this?'

'What have I done?' Margayya asked pathetically. He was beginning to feel very foolish. Society was pressing in upon him from all sides—the latest in the shape of this woman who had on her back a bundle of unwashed linen. Vegetable sellers, oil mongers, passers-by, cart-men, students—everyone seemed to have a right to talk to him as they pleased. Society seemed to overwhelm him on all sides. The lone cyclist was hardly an adequate support on which to lean. Margayya turned and looked for him. He too was gone. He saw his son clinging fast to the waist of the cucumber seller, sobbing and sobbing, and gaining more sympathizers. Margayya knew that the little boy would not let his sympathizers go until they took him to the shop across the road and bought him peppermints.

The crowd turned away and was now following Balu, and Margayya felt relieved that they were leaving him alone. He broke a twig off an avenue tree, and vaguely poked it into the gutter and ran the stick from end to end. He only succeeded in raising a stench. A schoolmaster who passed that way advised: 'Call a scavenger and ask him to look for it. He'll have the proper thing with him for poking here. Don't try to do everything yourself.' Margayya obediently dropped the stick into the drain, reflecting, 'No one will let me do what I like.' He turned to go back into his house. He climbed the steps with bowed head, because his brother's entire family was ranged along the wall on the other side. He quickly passed in. When he was gone they commented: 'Something is always agitating that household and creating a row.' Margayya went straight into the kitchen, where his wife was cooking, ignorant of all that had happened, and told her: 'The folk in the next house seem to have no better business than to hang about to see what is going on here . . . Do they ever find the time to cook, eat or sleep?' This was a routine question, needing no reply from his wife. She merely asked: 'Where is the child?' 'Probably rolling in the gutter,' he answered wearily. 'What has come over you?' she asked. 'You don't seem to be in your senses since last night.'

'I'm not. And if you try to imply that I have been drinking or spending the night in a brothel, I leave you free to think so—'

*

Margayya had converted the small room into a study for Balu. Every morning Margayya carried out an inspection of this room in order to see that his son learnt civilized ways and kept his things in their proper places, but he always found the mat not spread out on the floor, but stood up against a corner half-rolled, his books scattered on the floor, and his little desk full of stones, feathers, cigarette foils and empty packets. These were all collected from a small shop made of dealwood planks nearby which had recently been set up by a man from Malabar. Margayya felt unhappy when he saw the condition of this room. In his view a study had to be a very serious place, with books arrayed on one side, and the clothes of the scholar folded and in their place on the wire stretched across the wall. Margayya had secured a small framed picture of the goddess Saraswati, the goddess of learning and enlightenment, sitting beside her peacock and playing on the strings of a veena. He hung it in the study and enjoined his son ceremoniously to pray to the goddess every morning as soon as he got up from bed. He inquired untiringly, 'Boy, have you made your prostrations before the goddess?'

'Yes,' the boy answered, and ran in and performed them in a moment, then came back to the hall and just hung about staring at the sky or into the kitchen. Margayya felt angry. He told his son sharply: 'God is not like your drill class, to go and dawdle about half-heartedly. You must have your heart in it.'

'I prostrated all right, Father.'

'Yes, but your mind was where?'

'I was thinking of . . .' He considered for a moment, and added, 'my lessons,' knowing it would please his father. But it did not seem to have that effect.

'When you prostrate, you must not prostrate so fast.'

'How long can I lie on the floor prostrate?' the boy asked sullenly. 'I can't be lying there all the time.'

'If you grumble so much about your duties to the goddess, you will never become a learned man, that is all,' Margayya warned him.

'I don't care,' said the boy, very angry at the thought of an exacting goddess.

'You will be called a useless donkey by the whole world, remember,' Margayya said, his temper rising. 'Learn to talk with more reverence about the gods . . . Do you know where I was, how I started, how I earned the favour of the goddess by prayer and petition? Do you know why I succeeded? It was because my mind was concentrated on the goddess. The goddess is the only one who can—'

The boy cut him short with, 'I know it is a different goddess you worshipped. It is that Goddess Lakshmi. I know all that from Mother.'

Margayya felt upset by this taunt. He called his wife and asked, 'Why have you been talking nonsense to this boy? He is saying all sorts of things.'

'What has he been saying?' asked the wife, wiping her wet hands on the end of her saree.

Margayya was at a loss to explain. There was really no basis for his charge. He merely said, 'That boy contradicts me.' He turned furiously on his son and said, 'It is all the same goddess. There is no difference between Lakshmi and Saraswati, do you understand?'

The boy was not to be cowed. He simply said, 'They are different, I know.' He said it with an air of finality. Margayya asked, 'How do you know? Who told you?'

'My master.'

'Who? Murti? I will speak to that fool. If he is putting obstinate ideas into your head, he is not fit to be your teacher.' Then he added, 'Tell me as soon as he comes tomorrow or this evening.'

'But you won't be at home when he comes,' said the boy.

'Let him wait for me. Tell him he must see me,' said Margayya.

'All right,' said the boy. Margayya then ordered him out with, 'You can go and do your sums now. Don't waste the precious hours of the morning.' Balu ran off with great relief to his study and read a page out of his geography at the top of his voice so that all other sounds in the house were drowned.

He went to school trembling with the joyous anticipation of carrying a piece of unpleasant news to his teacher. The moment he sighted him he cried, 'Sir, sir, my father has asked you to wait for him this evening.'

The teacher's face turned pale. 'Why? Why?' he stammered nervously. There were some boys watching them, and he said, 'Go away boys, attend to your work, why do you stand and gape,' as sternly as he could. He then took Balu aside and said: 'Tell me boy, why does your father want me to see him?' 'I don't know, sir,' Balu replied, enjoying the occasion completely. 'I don't know, sir.' He shook his head, but his eyes were lively with mischief and suppressed information. The teacher tried to frighten him: 'Should you not ask him why he wants to when somebody says he wants to meet somebody else? Must you be taught all these elementary things?'

'Oh, my father cannot be asked all that. He will be very angry if he is questioned like that. Why should I be beaten by him, sir? Do you want me to be beaten by him, sir?'

The teacher took him privately under the tamarind tree and begged: 'See here, what exactly happened today, won't you tell me, won't you tell your teacher?'

He sounded melodramatic, and Balu started bargaining, 'I couldn't do any sums this morning.' The teacher assured him that he would condone the lapse. And then Balu went on to the next bargaining point by which the teacher himself should do the sums and not bother Balu except to the extent of showing him what marks he had obtained for them. When it was granted, Balu demanded: 'You promised me barfi; I must have it this afternoon, sir.'

'You will surely get a packet from me this afternoon,' said the teacher affably. After all this, Balu told him the reason why his father wanted to meet him. The teacher cried: 'I say, whatever made you speak thus? Have I ever mentioned to you anything about Lakshmi or anything of the kind?'

'My father asked who told me all that, and so I had to say it was you,' said Balu, with obscure logic.

The teacher waited for Margayya's arrival in the evening after finishing the lessons with Balu. Balu went in to demand his dinner. It was past eight when Margayya came home. As the pit-pat of his sandals were heard outside the teacher felt acutely uneasy and stood up. Margayya carefully put away his sandals in the corridor and came in. He saw the teacher and asked, 'What is the matter, teaching so late!' The teacher went forward officiously, rubbed his hands and said, 'Oh, I finished the lessons long ago, and Balu has even gone to sleep. I only waited to see you, sir,' he added.

'Oh, now, impossible,' said Margayya. He proceeded to put away his upper cloth and take off his shirt. 'I come home after a hard day's work and now you try to catch me for some idiotic school business, I suppose. Do you think I have no other business? Go, go, nothing doing now.'

'All right, sir,' the teacher said, turning to go, greatly relieved.

'Is there anything else?' Margayya shouted as the other was going. The teacher thought for a moment and said: 'Nothing special, sir,' in a most humble tone, which satisfied Margayya. His self-importance was properly fed; and so he said, as a sort of favour to the teacher, 'I hope Balu is all right?'

'Oh, yes, sir; he is quite up to the mark although he needs constant watching . . .'

'Well, as a teacher that is what you are expected to do, remember. And any time you see him getting out of hand, don't wait for me. Thrash him. Thrash him well.' As a sort of general philosophy, he added, 'No boy who has not been thrashed has come to any good. I am going to be extremely busy and won't have much time for anything. Don't take your eyes off the boy.'

'Yes, sir, I will always do my best; as a teacher my interest is to see him rise in the world as a man of—'

Margayya turned and went away to the backyard

without waiting for him to finish the sentence. His wife picked up a vessel of water and gave it to him. As he poured it over himself and she could be sure he was feeling cooler, she said, 'Why do you constantly say "thrash", "thrash" whenever you speak of the child? It is not good.'

Margayya replied, 'Oh, you believe it! It is just a formality with teachers, that is all. It keeps them in trim. After all, the fellow takes ten rupees a month and he must keep himself alert; but he dare not even touch our little darling. I would strike off that miserable teacher's head.'

It was all very bewildering to his wife. She asked, 'If you don't want him to do it why do you tell him to thrash him?'

'That is the way things have to be done in the world, my dear. If you see a policeman ask him to catch the thief, if you see a monkey ask him to go up a tree, and if you see a teacher ask him to thrash his pupil ... These are the things they do and it pleases them, they are appropriate. If you want to please me tell me to put up the interest, and I at once feel am being spoken to by a friend and well-wisher!'

NATARAJ'S PREDICAMENT

[In this excerpt from the novel The Man-eater of Malgudi, *Nataraj the printer finds himself in a fix when his house guest Vasu, a taxidermist, shoots a neighbour's dog in order to stuff it. What ensues is an amusing campaign to placate the dog's aged owner and find a possible replacement.]*

THE SEPTUAGENARIAN CAME along, tapping his stick; he stood in the road, looked up through his glasses, shading his eyes with one hand, and asked in a querulous voice, 'Is Nataraj in?' The usual crowd was there. 'Now is the testing time for Nehru,' the journalist was saying. 'If the Chinese on our border are not rolled back—' The poet had brought the next canto of his poem and was waiting to give me a summary of it. The septuagenarian asked again, 'Is Nataraj here?' unable to see inside owing to the glare.

'Yes, yes, I'm here,' I cried, and went down to help him up the steps.

He seated himself and looked at the other two. 'Your friends? I may speak freely, I suppose?' I introduced them to him, whereupon he expatiated on the qualities of a poet, and his duties and social relationships, and then turned to me with the business on hand. 'Nataraj, you know my grandson had a pet—a dog that he had kept for two years. He was very much devoted to it, and used to play with it the moment he came back from school.' I almost foresaw what was coming. 'Someone killed it last night. It lay under the street-lamp shot through the heart; someone seems to have shot it with a gun. Who has a gun here in these parts? I thought no one but the police had guns.'

'Why did you let it out?'

'Why? I don't know. It generally jumps over the wall and goes around the neighbourhood. It was a harmless dog, only barking all night, sitting under that street-lamp. I don't know what makes these dogs bark all night. They say that ghosts are visible to the eyes of a dog. Is it true? Do you believe in ghosts?'

'I haven't been able to see any,' I began.

'Oh, that's all right. Most people don't see them. Why should they? What was I saying?' he asked pathetically, having lost track of his own sentence. I was loath to remind him. I hesitated and wavered, hoping that he'd forget the theme of the dead dog and concentrate on the ghosts. But the journalist said, 'You were speaking about the dog, sir.'

'Ah, yes, yes. I could not bear to see its corpse, and so I asked the scavenger to take it away. I don't know what you call that breed. We called it Tom and it was black and hairy, very handsome; someone brought it from Bombay and gave it to my son, who gave it to this little fellow—quite a smart dog, very watchful, would make such a row if anyone tried to enter our gate, would wait for me to get up from my morning prayer, because he knew he would get a piece of the bread I eat in the morning. For the last three years doctors have ordered me to eat only bread, one slice of it. Before that I used to take idli every day, but they think it's not good for me. My father lived to be a hundred and never missed idli even for a single day.' He fell silent thinking of those days.

I was glad he was not asking to be reminded of his main theme. I hoped he would get up and go away. Everyone maintained a respectful, gloomy silence. If it had continued another minute, he would have risen and I'd have helped him down the steps. But just at the crucial moment Sastri came in with a proof for my approval. As soon as he entered by the curtain, instead of handing me the proof and disappearing he stood arrested for a minute, staring at the old man. 'What was all that commotion at your gate this morning? I was coming to the press and had no time to stop and ask. But I saw your grandchild crying.'

'Oh, is that you, Sastri?' asked the old man, shrinking his eyes to slits in order to catch his features. 'How are you, Sastri? It's many months since I saw you. What are you doing? Yes, of course I know you are working with Nataraj. How do you find his work, Nataraj? Good? Must be good. His uncle was my class-mate, and he had married the third daughter of . . . He used to come and play with my nephew. Where do you live, Sastri? Not near us?' Sastri mentioned his present address. 'Oh, that is far off Vinayak Street; ah, how many centuries it seems to me since I went that way. Come and see me some time, I'll be pleased.'

Sastri seemed pleased to be thus invited. He said, 'I must, I must come some time.'

'How many children have you?' Sastri mentioned the number, at which the old man looked gratified and said, 'Bring them along also when you come. I'd like to see them.'

Instead of saying 'Yes' and shutting up, Sastri said, 'Even this morning I could have come for a moment, but there was too much of a crowd at your gate.'

'Oh, idiot Sastri! What on earth are you becoming so loquacious for?' I muttered to myself. 'Leave him alone to forget this morning's crowd.'

But he had stirred up mischief. 'Didn't you know why there was a crowd?'

'No, I only saw your grandchild crying. I was in a hurry.'

The reminder of his grandchild nearly brought the septuagenarian to the verge of a breakdown. The old man almost sobbed, 'That boy is refusing to cheer up. I can't bear to see the youngster in such misery.'

'Why? Why? What happened?' asked Sastri.

'Someone had shot his pet dog,' said the journalist.

'Shot! Shot!' cried Sastri as if he had been poked with the butt of a rifle. 'When? Was it shot dead? Oh, poor dog! I have often seen it at your gate, the black one!' Why was he bent upon adding fuel to the fire? 'Do you know who could have shot it?' he asked menacingly.

'For what purpose?' said the old man. 'It's not going to help us. Will it bring Tom back to life?'

But Sastri insisted on enlightening him. He gave the old man the killer's name, whereabouts, and situation, and added, 'He is just the man who could have done it.'

The old man tapped his staff on the floor and shouted at me, 'And yet you said nothing? Why? Why?'

'It didn't occur to me, that is all,' I said hollowly. The old man tapped the floor with his staff and cried, 'Show me where he is, I'll deal with him. I'll hand him over to the police for shooting at things. What's your connection with him? Is he related to you? Is he your friend?' I tried to pacify the old man, but he ignored my words. 'In all my years, this is the first time I have heard of a shooting in our street. Who is this man? Why should you harbour him? Tomorrow he'll aim his gun at the children playing in the street!'

Knowing Vasu's style of speech with children, I could agree with the old man's views. The old man's hands and legs trembled, his face was flushed. I feared he might have a stroke and collapse in my press— anything seemed possible in my press these days. I said, 'Be calm, sir, it will not do to get excited. It's not good for you.'

'If it's not good for me, let me die. Why should anything be good for me? Death will be more welcome to me than the sight of my unhappy grandson.'

'I'll get him another dog, sir, please tell him that, a beautiful black one. I promise.'

'Can you?' asked the old man, suddenly calming down. 'Are you sure? You know where one is to be found?'

'Oh, yes,' I said, 'the easiest thing. I know many planters who have dogs, and I can always get a puppy for our little friend.'

'Will you accompany me now and say that to him?'

'Oh, surely,' I said, rising.

Sastri chose just this moment to thrust the proof before me and ask, 'Shall I put it on the machine?'

I didn't want anything to stop the old man from getting up and going, so I said, 'Wait a moment, I'll be back.' But Sastri would not allow me to go. 'If you pass this proof, we can print it off, everything is ready. They are shutting off power at eleven o'clock today. If we don't deliver . . .'

'Oh, Sastri, leave everything alone. I don't care what happens. I must see the child first and comfort him.' I was desperately anxious that the old man should be bundled off before someone or other should offer to point Vasu out to him.

*

Nothing happened for two days. I was in my usual chair one afternoon when Vasu's jeep pulled up at my door. My heart gave a thump. He sat in his jeep and said, 'Nataraj, come here.' I had an impulse to drop whatever I was doing, rush up to him and seize the chance to make friends with the monster again. But my pride was stronger. I suddenly resented all the trouble he had caused me. 'Come and speak if you have anything to say.' I was amazed at my own temerity.

He grinned, 'Ah, you are showing some spirit after all, that's good.'

I didn't like the paternal tone he adopted. I asked again, 'What is your business with me? I'm rather busy.'

'Yes, yes,' he said mockingly. 'I see it, and it's good

to see a man do an honest job at his office instead of chatting away the time with friends who treat the place as a club lounge.' This was a reference to my two friends who had come to see me after a long time. He went on shouting from his jeep, 'I appreciate your guts, Nataraj. I had thought that you were rather spineless. I now know that you have a spine. I'd never have dreamt that you would set that ghost in khaki on me! You were smart to think it up. So that's your move; you want to know what I'll do next?'

'No, I'm not interested. I'm busy.'

'You showed him the way to my room. He sees all the things there. What of it? Ask your friends to put a rubber-stamp on the backs of all the beasts in Mempi, so that he may identify them later and not make a fool of himself, and not make a fool of you either.' He drove off.

Sen said, 'I don't envy your luck in getting a man like that to live with.'

I wondered what Vasu's menacing words might mean. Legally he had trapped me at the Rent Controller's court, and the adjournment lawyer was handling the case, every now and then tapping me for a five or ten, but I found that he was satisfied even if I gave him just a couple of rupees, and made no mention of the money he owed me for printing his daughter's wedding card. I thought Vasu had done his worst, but now what did he mean? I hoped he was not planning to abduct my son and hold him to ransom. He might be up to anything. That evening I told my wife, 'If you have any urgent business to call me, wait till I come home. Don't send the little fellow across.'

She grew nervous and asked, 'Why?'

I just said, 'I don't want him to come there and make a fuss, that's all.'

'You see so little of him,' she complained, and added, 'You leave before he wakes, and come home after he is asleep, and if he wants to see his father he mustn't even come to the press, I suppose?' Then I had to explain and she grew really frightened.

She was in a panic. She kept the front door shut. She was completely demoralized if the boy did not come home at six. She behaved as if the monster would be unleashed and come rushing in to swallow up the family if the back door of my press was opened. My son seemed to enjoy the thrill of the situation as long as there was daylight. He spoke to his friends about the dangers that surrounded his life, and I saw batches of schoolboys standing around in knots in front of my press, looking up at the attic window during the afternoon recess at school. I became curious and beckoned to a couple of children to come in. 'What are you all doing here?'

'Nothing,' said one of them. 'We are going home from school.'

'What are you looking for?' I asked.

'Babu said there was, was . . . some giant here . . .'

'You want to look at him?' They nodded. 'Better not. Go home, boys. There is no such creature here.' I was anxious they should not see Vasu, as they might shout and circle round him and infuriate him. Knowing his attitude to children, I did not want to risk a meeting between them. One of them asked, slyly, 'Is it true that he eats dogs?'

'Oh, no,' I said immediately. 'He eats rice and other stuff just as we do. That's all false.'

'Then why did he shoot Ramu's dog?'

'Oh, that! It was shot by mistake. He was expecting a black bear and had his gun ready, but at the same time this dog came . . .'

'It was called Lily,' said one boy. The other contradicted, 'No, it was Tom.'

'No, it's Lily,' persisted the first. 'Yes, what'll you give me if it is Lily? Shall we go and ask Ramu?'

'Yes, come on,' and both ran off as if they were a couple of birds that had alighted at the window and were flying off. Two other children who were watching the scene also ran off happily shouting, 'Let us ask Ramu.'

My son came up with Ramu one afternoon two days later. Ramu said, 'My grandfather asked me to see you.' My son added, 'He has come to ask for his dog.'

Several weeks had gone by since I had promised the septuagenarian that I'd replace his grandson's dog. Although at that time it had seemed a perfectly feasible thing to find another dog, as days passed it began to look more and more difficult. I had promised in a moment of emotional stress, and now in the cold light of day it appeared to me an unreal, impossible task. I did not know how to acquire a puppy or where one was to be had. I had no doubt mentioned some planter with a dog. I had had in mind Achappa, a coffee planter on Mempi, for whose estates I used to do printing work at one time. I remembered his saying that he had a Great Dane pair with nine puppies. Did I need one? That was years ago. Achappa was not to be seen nowadays; occasionally his manager was observed at my neighbour's press.

I walked across to the Star Printers and said, 'If you see anyone from Consolidated Estates, please call me.' He replied that it was months since he had seen anyone from Consolidated Estates and suspected that Achappa was getting his printing done at Madras. So there it was. The dog-sources were drying up. I needed some expert help in the matter. My sincerity was unquestionable, but my resources were poor. I had no time either. Every day the boy came to my press and said, 'My grandfather asked me to see you.' And every day I gave him some reply and sent him off.

It was becoming a mechanical action. And the boy went away satisfied with any answer I gave. My intentions were absolutely honest, but the press work was heavy nowadays and I did not have a moment to spare. In addition to other work Sen was giving me manifestos to print and the poet was fetching his cantos with greater speed. With one thing and another my time flew swiftly each day. I had to work hard and make enough money at least to pay the lawyer whenever he held his hand out for cash! I had not given up hopes of recovering my dues from him, but I obeyed his advice not to mix up accounts.

I had no time actually to go out and seek a dog for the boy, but I had several plans in my head. I'd make a list of all my friends with dogs, tabulate each breed, note down their breeding time, make one of them promise to give one of the litter to me, make a round of visits every Sunday afternoon, and finally pick up a dog for the young fellow. My son asked me at nights while he nestled close to me (when night advanced the fear of the monster grew in him and he refused to sleep in a separate bed), as if he were a sharer of my dream, 'Get me a puppy too, Father, when you get one for Ramu.'

'Yes, yes,' I said. 'Why not?'

THE FRAMING SHOP ON
MARKET ROAD

*[Originally titled 'Uncle', this short story chronicles
a day's adventures for a child as he ventures out
with his uncle, culminating in his being lost on the
streets of Malgudi late at night.]*

I AM THE monarch of all I survey, being the sole
occupant of this rambling ancient house in Vinayak
Street. I am five feet ten, too huge for the easy chair
on which I am reclining now. But I remember the time
when I could hardly reach the arm of this easy chair.
I remember the same chair at the same spot in the hall,
with some ancient portrait hanging on a nail over it,
and my uncle comfortably lounging and tormenting me
by pushing his glittering snuffbox just out of my reach.
While trying to reach for it I tumbled down again and
again; he emitted a loud guffaw each time I lost my
balance and sprawled on the floor. I felt frightened by

his loud laughter and whined and cried. At that moment my aunt would scoop down on me and carry me off to the kitchen, set me down in a corner, and place before me a little basin filled with water, which I splashed about. I needed no further attention except a replenishment of water from time to time. I also watched with wonderment the smoke curling up from the oven when the lady puffed her cheeks and blew on the fire through a hollow bamboo pipe. The spell would suddenly be broken when she picked me up again, with a bowl of rice in her hand, and carried me off to the street door. She would carefully seat me on the pyol of the house, my back supported against the slender pillars, and try to feed me. If I averted my head she gripped my neck as in a vise and forced the rice between my lips. If I howled in protest she utilized the chance to thrust more rice into my open mouth. If I spat it out she would point at a passer-by and say, 'See that demon, he will carry you off. He is on the lookout for babies who won't eat.' At that stage I must have faced the risk of dying of over- rather than under-feeding. Later in the day she would place a dish of eatables before me and watch me deal with it. When I turned the dish over on the floor and messed up the contents, Uncle and Aunt drew each other's attention to this marvellous spectacle and nearly danced around me in joy. In those days my uncle, though portly as ever, possessed greater agility, I believe.

My uncle stayed at home all day. I was too young to consider what he did for a living. The question never occurred to me until I was old enough to sit on a school bench and discuss life's problems with a class fellow. I was studying in the first year at Albert Mission School. Our teacher had written on the blackboard a set of words such as Man, Dog, Cat, Mat, Taj and Joy, and had asked us to copy them down on our slates and take them to him for correction and punishment if necessary. I had copied four of the six terms and had earned the teacher's approbation. The boy in the next seat had also done well. Our duties for the hour were over, and that left us free to talk, in subdued whispers, though.

'What is your uncle's name?' he asked.

'I don't know. I call him Uncle.'

'Is he rich?' the boy asked.

'I don't know,' I replied. 'They make plenty of sweets at home.'

'Where does he work?' asked the boy, and the first thing I did when I went home, even before flinging off my books and school bag, was to ask loudly, 'Uncle, where is your office?'

He replied, 'Up above,' pointing heavenward, and I looked up.

'Are you rich?' was my second question.

My aunt emerged from the kitchen and dragged me in, saying, 'Come, I have some very lovely things for you to eat.'

I felt confused and asked my aunt, 'Why won't Uncle . . .?' She merely covered my mouth with her palm and warned, 'Don't talk of all that.'

'Why?' I asked.

'Uncle doesn't like to be asked questions.'

'I will not ask hereafter,' I said and added, 'Only that Suresh, he is a bad boy and he said . . .'

'Hush,' she said.

*

My world was circumscribed by the boundaries of our house in Vinayak Street, and peopled by Uncle and Aunt mainly. I had no existence separately from my uncle. I clung to him all through the day. Mornings in the garden at the backyard, afternoons inside, and all evening on the front pyol of the house squatting beside him. When he prayed or meditated at midday I sat in front of him watching his face and imitating him. When he saw me mutter imaginary prayers with my eyes shut, he became ecstatic and cried aloud to my aunt in the kitchen, 'See this fellow, how well he prays! We must teach him some slokas. No doubt whatever, he is going to be a saint someday. What do you think?'

When he prostrated to the gods in the puja room I too threw myself on the floor, encouraged by the compliments showered on me. He would stand staring at me until Aunt reminded him that his lunch was ready. When he sat down to eat I nestled close to him, pressing my elbow on his lap. Aunt would say, 'Move off, little man. Let Uncle eat in peace,' but he always countermanded her and said, 'Stay, stay.' After lunch he chewed betel leaves and areca nut, moved on to his bedroom, and stretched himself on his rosewood bench, with a small pillow under his head. Just when he fell into a doze I demanded, 'Tell me a story,' butting him with my elbow.

He pleaded, 'Let us both sleep. We may have wonderful dreams. After that I will tell you a story.'

'What dreams?' I would persist.

'Shut your eyes and don't talk, and you will get nice dreams.' And while I gave his advice a trial, he closed his eyes.

All too brief a trial. I cried, 'No, I don't see any dream yet. Tell me a story, Uncle.' He patted my head and murmured, 'Once upon a time . . .' with such a hypnotic effect that within a few minutes I fell asleep.

Sometimes I sought a change from the stories and involved him in a game. The bench on which he tried to sleep would be a mountain top, the slight gap between its edge and the wall a gorge with a valley below. I would crawl under the bench, lie on my back, and command, 'Now throw,' having first heaped at his side a variety of articles such as a flashlight without battery, a ping-pong bat, a sandalwood incense holder, a leather wallet, a coat hanger, empty bottles, a tiny stuffed cow, and several other items out of a treasure chest I possessed. And over went the most cherished objects—the more fragile the better for the game, for, in the cool semi-dark world under the bench and by the rules of the game, the possibility of a total annihilation of objects would be perfectly in order.

Ten days after first broaching the subject Suresh cornered me again when we were let off for an hour in the absence of our geography master. We were playing marbles. Suresh suddenly said, 'My father knows your uncle.'

I felt uneasy. But I had not learnt the need for circumspection and asked anxiously, 'What does he say about him?'

'Your uncle came from another country, a far-off place . . .'

'Oh, good, so?' I cried with happiness, feeling relieved that after all some good points about my uncle were emerging.

Suresh said, 'But he impersonated.'

'What is "impersonate"?' I asked.

He said, 'Something not so good. My mother and

father were talking, and I heard them use the word.'

The moment I came home from school and flung off my bag my aunt dragged me to the well in the backyard and forced me to wash my hands and feet, although I squirmed and protested vehemently. Next I sat on the arm of my uncle's easy chair with a plate filled with delicacies, ever available under that roof, and ate under the watchful eye of my uncle. Nothing delighted him more than to eat or watch someone eat. 'What is the news in your school today?' he would ask.

'Know what happened, Uncle?' I swallowed a mouthful and took time to suppress the word 'impersonate', which kept welling up from the depths of my being, and invent a story. 'A bad boy from the Third B—big fellow—jabbed me with his elbow . . .'

'Did he? Were you hurt?'

'Oh, no, he came charging but I stepped aside and he banged his head against the wall, and it was covered with blood, and they carried him to the hospital.' My uncle uttered many cries of joy at the fate overtaking my adversary and induced me to develop details, which sounded gory.

When they let me go I bounced off to the street, where a gang awaited my arrival. We played marbles or kicked a rubber ball about with war cries and shouts, blissfully unaware of the passers-by and the traffic, until the street end melted into a blaze of luminous dust with the sun gone. We played until my uncle appeared at our doorway and announced, 'Time to turn in,' when we dispersed unceremoniously and noisily. Once again my aunt would want to give my hands and feet a scrubbing. 'How many times!' I protested, 'Won't I catch a cold at this rate?'

She just said, 'You have all the road dust on you now. Come on.' After dousing me she smeared sacred ash on my forehead and made me sit with my uncle in the back veranda of the house and recite holy verses. After which I picked up my school books and, under my uncle's supervision, read my lessons, both the tutor and the taught feeling exhausted at the end of it. By eight-thirty I would be fed and put to sleep in a corner of the hall, at the junction of the two walls where I felt most secure.

On Fridays we visited the little shrine at the end of our street. Rather an exciting outing for me, as we passed along brilliantly-lit shops displaying banana bunches, coloured drinks, bottled peppermints, and red and yellow paper kites, every item seeming to pulsate with an inner glow.

*

They both rose at five in the morning and moved about softly so as not to disturb me. The first thing in the day, my uncle drew water from the well for the family, and then watered the plants in the garden. I woke to the sound of the pulley creaking over the well and joined my uncle in the garden. In the morning light he looked like a magician. One asked for nothing more in life than to be up at that hour and watch brilliant eddying columns of water coming through little channels dug along the ground. The hydraulic engineering for the garden was my uncle's own. He had raised the ground beside the well to form a basin, and when he tipped a cauldron of water over it, the column ran down the slope and passed through to the plants according to his dictates. He controlled the supply of water at various stages with a little trowel in hand, with which he scooped up the mud and opened or blocked the water course. I floated little bits of straw or leaves, or picked up ants and helped them have a free swim along the current. Sometimes without my uncle's knowledge I scooped off the mud bank with my hands and diverted the water elsewhere.

I revelled in this world of mud, greens, slush and water, forgetting for the moment such things as homework and teachers. When the sun came over the walls of the house behind our garden, my uncle ended his operations, poured a great quantity of water over himself, and went in dripping, in search of a towel. When I tried to follow him in, my aunt brought out a bucket of hot water and gave me a bath beside the well. Soon I found myself in the puja room murmuring prayers.

A perpetual smell of incense and flowers hung about the puja room, which was actually an alcove in the kitchen where pictures of gods hung on the walls. I loved the pictures: the great God Krishna poised on the hood of a giant serpent; Vishnu, blue-coloured, seated on the back of Garuda, the divine eagle, gliding in space and watching us. As I watched the pictures my mind went off into fantastic speculations while my tongue recited holy verses. 'Was the eagle a sort of aeroplane for Vishnu? Lakshmi stands on a lotus! How can anyone stand on a lotus flower without crushing it?' From the fireplace would come my aunt's voice, 'I don't hear you pray.' I would suppress my speculations and recite aloud, addressing the elephant-faced god, '*Gajananam bhutaganadi sevitam . . .*' for three minutes in Sanskrit. I always wanted to ask for its meaning, but if I paused my aunt would shout over the hissing of the frying pan (which, incidentally, was generating an enormously appetizing fragrance), 'Why have you stopped?' Now I would turn to the picture of Saraswati, the goddess of learning, as she sat on a rock with her peacock beside a cool shrubbery, and wonder at her ability to play the veena with one hand while turning the rosary with the other, still leaving two hands free, perhaps to pat the peacock. I would raise my voice and say, '*Saraswati namastubhyam*', which meant 'O goddess of learning, I bow to you,' or some such thing. I secretly added a personal request to this prayer. 'May you help me get through my school hours without being mauled by my teachers or other boys, may I get through this day unscathed.' Although my normal day at school was peaceful, I always approached it at the beginning of each day with dread. My teacher was unshaved and looked villainous. He frequently inhaled a pinch of snuff in the class and spoke in a grating voice, the snuff having ravaged his vocal cords, and he flourished a short, stubby cane menacingly at the whole class every now and then. I had never seen him attack anyone, but his gestures were frightening, and I sat on my bench shuddering lest he should turn in my direction and notice me.

My life was precisely organized by my uncle, and I had little time to waste. When I emerged from the puja I had to go straight to the kitchen and drink off a glass of milk. This would be an occasion for my aunt to comment on my dress or voice. She would suddenly bring her face close to mine and examine my eyes. 'What are you looking for?' I would ask, rearing my head, but she held it firmly between her palms and inspected until she was satisfied that there was no patch of dirt or swelling under my eyes. 'Oh, I was mistaken, nothing,' she would say with relief. 'Anyway, you have grown darker. You must not roast yourself in the sun so much. Why should they make you do all that drill in the sun?'

Next I passed into the jurisdiction of my uncle, who sat leaning against a pillar in the hall with eyes shut in meditation. He said, emerging from his trance, 'Boy, gather all your lessons for the day and put them in your bag. Have you sharpened your pencil? Cleaned your slate? Do you need anything?' In spite of my firm statement that I needed nothing, he came over, seized my school bag, peered into it, and probed its bottom with his fingers. It was surprising how lightly he could abandon his prayers, but he was perhaps an adept who could resume them at will, as his day was mostly divided between munching and meditation. He held up to the light a slate pencil in order to judge whether it could be used for just another day. He would sharpen its point on the stone floor, commenting, 'You must hold it here and write, and don't bite the end; this can be used for a week more.' It was painful to write with such a short stub; my thumb and forefinger became sore, and further, if my teacher noticed it he twisted my ear and snatched away the stub and made me stand on the bench as a punishment. I could not mention these problems explicitly, as I feared that my uncle might don his shirt and offer to visit my school in order to investigate. I had a secret anxiety lest he should ever appear in our school, as I thought that the boys might stand around and make fun of his girth. And so I had to manage with the stub as ordained. When he felt satisfied that I had used the pencil wisely, he would open his wooden cupboard, take out a lacquered casket with a dragon on its lid, and out of it a small cardboard box, and again from it a little package containing long slate pencils; he would take out a brand-new one and hesitate; guessing his intention, I would jump up and snatch it from his hand crying, 'Don't break it, I want it full-length.' Sometimes he gave it whole, sometimes he broke it into two saying, 'Half is long enough.' He then looked through my books page by page, and packed them securely back into the bag. He said from time to time, 'Little man, if you don't read your lessons properly you will never count for anything in life and no one will respect you. Do you understand?' 'Yes, Uncle,' I said, though not very clear in my mind as to what 'respect' meant.

*

One evening I came home announcing, 'They are going to photograph us in our school.' My uncle, who had been lounging in the easy chair, sprang to his feet and asked 'Who? Who is going to photograph you?'

'My teacher's brother has a friend who has a camera and he is going to photograph us.'

'Only you or others also?'

'Our class alone, not even the B section will be allowed, although they asked to be photographed too.'

Uncle's face lit up with joy. He called Aunt and said, 'Did you hear, this young man is going to be photographed tomorrow. Dress him properly.'

Next day my uncle spent a lot of time selecting clothes for me, and my aunt gave a double rub to my face and groomed me. My uncle followed me about uttering several pieces of advice before letting me out. 'You must never scowl even if the sun hits you in the eyes. You must try to look pleasant. You know in those days only girls waiting to be married used to have their photos taken. Nowadays everyone is being photographed.'

When I came home from school that evening he asked anxiously, 'How did it go off?'

I flung away the school bag to its corner and said, 'No, nothing happened. He didn't come.'

'Who?'

'Our teacher's brother's friend,' I said. 'It seems his camera has broken down or something like that, and so—no photo.'

My uncle's face fell. Both of them had been waiting at the door to see me return triumphantly from the photographer. He murmured sympathetically, 'Don't worry about it, we will find another photographer; only I thought you should not have taken out the blue shirt until Deepavali—never mind; we will buy you a new one for the festival.'

My aunt said, 'We could fold the shirt neatly and put it away until Deepavali. He has not soiled it.'

'I sat very quietly today lest the clothes should be spoilt,' I said, which was a fact. I had refused to play with my friends for fear that my shirt might get crumpled. This blue shirt was of a special kind; my uncle had bought the cloth from a street hawker, who assured him that the fabric was foreign and could not normally be acquired except through smugglers operating in certain coastal villages. Uncle bought three yards of the blue cloth after a whole afternoon's haggling, and planned to stitch shirts for me and himself. He had sent for an old Muslim tailor who had the original Singer sewing machine set up on the pyol of a house in Kabir Lane. He behaved extremely deferentially before my uncle and would not be seated even on the floor. My uncle relaxed in his easy chair and my aunt stood at the kitchen doorway and both discussed with the tailor various matters relating to persons, times, and places which sounded remote and incomprehensible to me. He kept addressing my uncle as his saviour at the end of every sentence, and salaamed him. When the time came to take measurements my uncle stood very erect and muttered numerous instructions as to the length, cut, and number and kind (unbreakable, tin) of buttons that he favoured, and so forth. 'Note the measurements down properly,' he said sternly several times, 'lest you should forget and make a mistake; it is a rare kind of cloth, not obtainable in our country; can't afford to take chances with it, remember.'

The tailor in answer avowed again his indebtedness to my uncle. 'On the road that day if you had not—' he began.

My uncle looked embarrassed and cut him short with, 'Don't go on with all those grandmother's stories now. The past is past, remember.'

'How can I help it, sir? Every morning my children and I think of you and pray for your welfare. When they gave me up for dead with vultures circling above and passed on, you stopped by and revived me, sir, although you had this baby in your arms ... and you gave me the strength to walk a thousand miles over mountain passes ...'

My uncle said curtly, 'Why don't you take the measurements?'

'I obey,' said the tailor immediately, and proceeded to measure me. He was not only deferential but also patronizing in his tone. 'Stand up, little master, otherwise you will blame this old man for any mistake that may occur. See how your venerable uncle stands erect at his age!'

He completed the measurements, noted them on a very small roll of paper, probably the torn-off margin of a newspaper, with a stubby pencil which he always carried over his ear, and departed after accepting all the advice given as they kept saying, 'Remember he is a growing boy, make allowance for that; don't want him to feel suffocated in his new shirt after the first wash ...'

The tailor left after uttering the only word of protest, 'If master had bought just a quarter yard more ...'

'Not at all necessary,' said my uncle. 'I know how much is needed, seeing that you are going to give me short arms, and no collar is wanted ...' The shirts came back stitched in due course and were laid away in the big trunk.

*

Next evening I came home gleefully announcing, 'We were photographed today.'

'Indeed!' cried my uncle. 'How stupid of them when you were not ready for it!'

'Does it mean that you are going to look like this in the photo?' asked my aunt.

'It will not do justice to you,' said my uncle. 'They should have given us at least half-an-hour's notice, and then you could have . . .'

'Our teacher suddenly said, "Come out, all of you, and stand in a line under the tree." We marched out. A man came with a small camera, lined up all the tall boys first and all the short ones in the second line with our teachers in the centre; and then he cried, "Stand steady, don't move," and it was over. Our teacher has promised to give a photo to whoever brings two rupees from home.'

'Two rupees!' repeated my uncle aghast.

Aunt said, 'Never mind, it is the child's first photo.'

'I thought the class would be let off after the photo, but we were marched back for geography lessons.'

My uncle thrust two rupees into my pocket before I left for school next day, cautioning me, 'Take it carefully to your teacher.' He sounded anxious lest I should drop the money or get robbed on the way. He stood on the front step and watched me go. I turned around a couple of times to assure him, 'Don't fear, I will be careful,' dreading lest he should suddenly don his shirt and decide to escort me.

For two weeks there was no sign of the photo. My uncle got quite agitated and asked every day, 'What did your teacher say?' I had to invent an answer each time as I did not have the courage to confront my teacher on the subject. And so I generally said, 'The photographer has been very ill. But tomorrow positively we are getting it.'

Ultimately the photo did arrive and we were given our copies at the end of the day. As I reached home I shouted from the street, 'Photo!' which brought my uncle down the steps of the house. He followed me anxiously about while I took my own time to fish out the photograph from my school bag. 'Such a small one!' my uncle cried on seeing it.

'His camera also was small!' I said.

They carried the print to a corner where a beam of sunlight streamed in through the red pane of a ventilator and observed it closely. Uncle put his spectacles on, but my aunt had to wait for her turn since they managed with a single pair between them. 'Why can't we go out, it is brighter out there, and I won't need glasses?' she suggested.

'No,' he replied firmly. 'Inquisitive fellows all around—fellows ready to peer through the wall if they could, to learn what is happening here,' said my uncle, putting on his spectacles and commenting, 'Our boy has the brightest face in the group, but they have made him look so dark!'

I pointed out my enemies to them: 'This is Suresh—always trying to kill me if I am not careful. This boy also is a bad fellow.' My aunt's eyes met mine significantly at the mention of Suresh, who looked florid by the red light of the ventilator. 'This is our teacher. He will not hesitate to skin alive anyone who is found talking in his class. The man who took the photo is his brother's friend. Own brother, not cousin. Suresh asked if he was a cousin, and it made my teacher so wild!'

My uncle counted the heads and cried, 'Fifty? Two rupees each and they have collected their one hundred rupees! Not even a mount for the photo! They are robbing us in your schools nowadays!'

Next day when I was leaving for school my uncle said, 'Come home early. We will go out to the market. Have you any important lessons?'

'None,' I said with conviction. 'I will come home for lunch and stay on.'

'Do you wish to come with us?' he asked, aiming his question in the direction of his wife in the kitchen. My aunt, with her years of experience behind her, flung back the responsibility of a decision on him, shouting from the fireplace, 'Do you want me to go with you?' The man was cornered now and answered, 'Not if you have things to mind at home ...'

'Of course, I have asked that servant woman to come and pound the paddy today. If we miss her today she will not come again.' She trailed off indecisively. This was a diplomatic game which, in spite of my age of innocence, I understood very well, and so I broke in. 'Let Aunt come another day, Uncle, she will want a carriage to be brought and all that trouble,' which was a fact; whenever she wanted to go out she would send me running to the street corner to fetch a jutka, and it was not always an easy job. Some days you found six jutkas waiting for fares under the margosa shade at the street corner, some days you couldn't find even one at a busy hour; sometimes the jutka drivers who knew me would tease and not take me seriously or pass disparaging remarks about my uncle, referring to him as 'that Rangoon man' or mention incidents which I could not comprehend, and generally mumble and smirk among themselves at my expense.

My uncle added, 'Quite right. We can walk to the market.'

'Yes, by all means,' said my aunt, much to everyone's relief.

We sallied out at three o'clock in the afternoon, having finished our tiffin and coffee. The main job for the day was to mount and frame the photograph. Uncle carried it in his hand delicately, enclosed in an old envelope, as if it were fragile and likely to perish at a finger's pressure. As we went down the street a neighbour standing at his door hailed us and demanded, 'Where are you taking the young fellow?' He was an engineer who worked in some distant projects on the hills, coming home once in a while and then again disappearing from our society. He was a particular friend of my uncle as they occasionally gathered for a game of cards in my house. He asked, 'I am here for a few days, can't we have a session sometime?'

'Of course, of course,' said my uncle without much fervour, 'I will let you know,' and moved on.

'Won't Aunt get angry?' I asked, remembering the arguments they had had after every card session. The card players would have been sitting around in the middle of the hall, demanding coffee and edibles, and playing far into the night. My aunt would complain after the company had dispersed, 'Sitting there with your friends, you lock me up in the kitchen all day! What madness seizes you people when you touch a pack of cards, I wonder!' Worn out by her attacks, my uncle began to avoid his friends, the company gradually dwindled and disappeared. But it did not prevent them from dreaming about cards or luxuriating in visions of a grand session. Somewhere my uncle was supposed to have lost a lot of money through the card games, and my aunt was very definite that he should never go near cards again, although he kept saying, 'We play only Twenty-eight, and not Rummy, after all, Twenty-eight . . .'

'Twenty-eight or forty-eight, it's all the same to me,' said my aunt. 'Fifty thousand rupees just scattered like waste paper, that is all! Sheer madness!' She was rather emphatic. My uncle, not being a quarrelsome sort, just accepted meekly whatever she said, and evidently benefited by her advice.

As we walked on I asked many questions. This was my opportunity to clear my doubts and learn about new things in life. I asked, 'Why does not Aunt like playing cards? So many nice people gather in our house and it is so interesting!'

He answered, 'It is very expensive, my boy, some people have lost all their fortune and become beggars. Gambling is bad. Don't you know how Nala lost his kingdom?' And he began to narrate the ancient story of Nala. Cyclists passed, a herd of cattle returned from the grazing fields beyond the river, some very young school children emerged from the town primary school, the sun scorching us all. But my uncle noticed nothing while he unfolded to me the fate of Nala, holding me by the wrist lest I should be run over or gored by the cattle. I shrank behind him when we passed my school. I had skipped three classes in the afternoon and did not wish to be seen by my teachers or classmates. We could hear the voices from within the classrooms. Presently the bell for the three-thirty recess would sound and the boys would rush out to drink water at the tap or to make water on the roadside or swarm around the groundnut seller at the school gate. The headmaster was likely to prowl about to prevent the boys from fouling the road. It would be disaster for me to be seen by anyone now. Nor did I wish my uncle to get any ideas while passing the gate—such as stopping to have a word with my teacher. I quickened my steps and tried to divert his mind to other matters by suddenly saying, 'Why did Nala lose?'

Before answering he paused for a moment to ask, 'Is that noise all from your school? Why do they make all that row? Glad we don't live next door to your school!' Not wanting him to dwell too much on school matters, I trotted ahead of him, hoping to set the pace for him. But he remarked, 'Do you have to caper like that? No, my boy, I could have given you a beating five years ago, but today I am deliberately slowing my pace.' I paused for him to catch up with me. We had crossed the danger zone, gone past the school.

I asked innocently as we resumed our march, 'What game did Nala play? Did he play cards?'

'Oh no,' Uncle said. 'I am sure he would have, if they had invented playing cards in those days. He played dice.' He went on to explain the game to me and continued the story, 'The fellow played with his brother, but malevolent gods had got into the dice and affected his chances, and he lost his kingdom and everything except his wife and had to march out of the capital like a mendicant wearing only a loincloth.'

We turned to our right and took a short cut

through Kabir Street and were on Market Road. Not a busy hour, as the high school boys were still not let off. Several donkeys stood about the fountain statuesquely. When the boys emerged from the high school, I imagined, they would shout and frighten the donkeys, provoke them in various ways until they ran helter-skelter, confusing the evening traffic. Street dogs dozing on the edge of the road would join the fray and give them chase, and there would be a hullabaloo. I missed all this imagined spectacle and told my uncle, 'We should have come a little later.'

'Why?' asked my uncle and added, 'You wish that you had attended your classes after all?'

'Oh, no,' I said, and blurted out, 'We could have seen the donkeys jump about.' Even without this spectacle Market Road thrilled me every inch, so full of life, movement, and activity. A candy peddler was crying his wares, sounding a bell. This man often established himself at our school gate, drawing out and pinching off portions of a pink, elastic, gluey sweet, stuck in a coil around a bamboo shaft. My mouth watered at the sight of it. I pleaded, 'Uncle, please get me a bit of it!'

He suddenly looked serious and said, 'No, no, it is dangerous to eat such stuff. You may catch cholera.'

I said with bravado, 'Not likely. He comes to our school every day, and all boys eat it, and also our drawing master. No one has suffered from cholera yet.'

All that he said was, 'I will get you something nicer to eat. Wait.' As we passed a sweetmeat shop he said, 'This is Jagan's shop. No harm in eating here. He makes things out of pure ghee.' He stopped by the resplendently-arrayed sweetmeat shop and bought a packet for me.

I swiftly unpacked it and asked out of courtesy, 'Uncle, you want some?' and when he shook his head I ate it, and threw away the wrapper high up and watched it gently floating down on Market Road until Uncle pulled me up, saying, 'Look in front and walk.'

The frame-maker's name was Jayraj. He had hoisted a signboard which was rather pompously worded 'Photographers & Photo-framers', stretching the entire width of the outer wall of the market. Why he chose to display himself in the plural no one could say, since no one ever saw anyone except Mr Jayraj in the proprietor's seat in the inner sanctum. Although there was always a goodly company on the long bench sticking out from his threshold, they were all his friends, well-wishers, customers, and general listeners, for Jayraj held forth on his social and personal philosophy all day. Now he gestured to us to be seated on the bench while he went on gently hammering tacks onto the sides of a frame covered with a cardboard. Presently he looked up and greeted my uncle, 'Doctor, where have you been all these days?'

I was surprised at my uncle being addressed as a doctor. Immediately I looked up and asked, 'Uncle, are you a doctor?' He merely rumpled my hair and did not answer.

Jayraj took this occasion to look at me and say, 'Brought this young man along, who is he?'

My uncle simply said, 'He is my boy, our child at home.'

'Oh, I know, yes of course, now grown up so!'

My uncle looked slightly awkward and changed the subject. He held out my photograph and asked with affected cheer, 'Oh, here is this young man's photo which must be framed. Will you do it?'

'Of course, anything for you, sir.' He looked at the photo with disgust. I thought he might fling the picture into the gutter that flowed copiously below the steps of his shop. His brow was furrowed, he pursed his lips, blinked his eyes, placed a straight finger across the picture, shook his head dolefully, and said, 'This is how people cheat schoolboys nowadays. Underexpose and overdevelop or overexpose and underdevelop. This is what they do.'

My uncle added fuel to the fire by saying, 'Not even a mount for the two rupees charged!'

Jayraj put away the photograph and said, 'Well,

mounting and framing is my duty, even if you bring the photo of a donkey's rear.' While he paused for breath my uncle tried to say something, but Jayraj didn't give him the chance. He said, 'Here I am in the heart of the city ready to serve our townfolk. Why can't people make use of me instead of some tenth-rate camera-meddler? I am open twenty-four hours of the day in the service of humanity. I even sleep here when there is work to do, and no factory act applies to me. I can't demand overtime or bonus, but my satisfaction lies in serving humanity.' He pointed at his camera, a hooded apparatus on a tripod in a corner. 'There it is, always ready. If somebody summons me I respond immediately, no matter what the subject is—a wedding, a corpse, a prostitute, a minister of state, or a cat on a wall—it's all the same to me. My business is to photograph, and let me tell you straight away that my charges are more than moderate. I don't believe in doing cheap work. I photographed Mahatma Gandhi when he was here. I was summoned to Madras whenever Nehru was on a visit. Dr Radhakrishnan, Tagore, Birla, I could give you a big list of people who were pleased with my work and wrote out testimonials spontaneously. I have locked them in the safe at home. Any day you will be welcome to visit my humble home and peruse them if you like. I don't mind losing all my gold, but not the testimonials from the brilliant sons of our motherland.

I want my children and their children to cherish them and say some day, "We come of a line who served the brilliant sons of Mother India, and here are the tokens." '

While this preamble was going on, his hands were busy giving the finishing touches to a wedding group; he was smoothing off the ripples of glue on the back of the picture. He squatted on his heels on the floor with a little workbench in front of him. He held the wedding group at arm's length and said, 'Not my business, so many committing the folly every week, the government looking on, while people howl about the population problem, but why can't they ban all marriages for ten years?' He packed the framed picture in an old newspaper, tied a string around it, and put it away. Now my turn. He picked up my photograph, studied it again, and remarked, 'Fifty heads to be compressed on a postcard. Maybe they are only little men, but still . . . Unless you look through a magnifying glass you will never know who is who.' He then asked my uncle, 'Will you leave the colour of the mount, frame, and style entirely to me or have you any ideas?'

My uncle was bewildered by this question and said, 'I want it to look nice, that is all. I want it to look,' he repeated, 'particularly nice.'

'I don't doubt it,' said Jayraj, who never liked the other person to end a conversation. 'Well, for the tone of this print there are certain shades of wooden frames and mounts suitable, and some not suitable. If you prefer something unsuitable according to me, it'll still be done. I will wrap it up, present it to you, and collect my bill; but let me assure you that my heart will not be in it. Anyway, it is up to you,' he said challengingly. My uncle seemed bewildered by all this philosophy and remained silent. He looked apprehensive and wanted to know the worst quickly. The man had placed my photograph on his desk, weighting it down with a steel measuring scale. We awaited his next move. Meanwhile more people came and took their seats on the bench, like men at a dentist's parlour. Jayraj did not bother to notice his visitors, nor did he notice the crowd passing through the market gateway, shoppers, hawkers, beggars, dogs and stray cattle and coolies with baskets on their heads, all kinds of men and women, jostling, shouting, laughing, cursing, and moving as in a mass trance; they might have been able to pass in and out more easily but for Jayraj's bench sticking across the market entrance.

A very bald man came and gingerly sat down on the bench, announcing, 'The trustee has sent me.' It made no impression on Jayraj, who had picked up a length of framing rod and was sawing it off noisily.

My uncle asked suddenly, 'When will you give it?'

Before Jayraj could muster an answer the bald man said for the fourth time, 'The trustee has sent me . . .'

Jayraj chose this moment to tell some other young man leaning on a bicycle, 'Tomorrow at one o'clock.' The young man jumped on his bicycle and rode away.

The bald man began again. 'The trustee . . .'

Jayraj looked at my uncle and said, 'It all depends on when you want it.'

The bald man said, 'The trustee . . . is going away to Tirupati tomorrow . . . and wants . . .'

Jayraj completed his sentence for him, 'Wants me along? Tell him I have no time for a pilgrimage.'

'No, no, he wants the picture.'

'Where is the hurry? Let him come back from Tirupati.'

The other looked nonplussed.

Meanwhile a woman who sold betel leaves in the market came up with a basket at her hip and asked, 'When should I bring the baby?'

'Whenever the midwife advises,' replied Jayraj. She blushed and threw the end of her sari over her face and laughed. 'Tomorrow evening at three o'clock. Dress him in his best. Put on him all the jewellery you can, and come early. If you come late the sunlight will be gone and there will be no photo. Be sure to bring two rupees with you. No credit, and then you can give me the balance when I give you the photo in a frame.'

'Ah, can't you trust me so much, sir?'

'No argument, that is my system, that is all. If I

want the betel leaves in your basket I pay for it at once, so also for what I do.' She went away laughing, and Jayraj said, addressing no one in particular, 'She has a child every ten months. Mother is constant, but not the father.' His assembly laughed at this quip. 'Not my business to question the parentage. I take the picture and frame it when ordered to do so and that is all.'

My uncle asked all of a sudden, 'Will you be able to frame and give me the photograph now?'

'No,' said Jayraj promptly, 'unless you expect me to stay on and work until midnight.'

'Why not? You said you could.'

'Yes sir,' he replied. 'I said so and I will say so again, if you command me. Will you wait and take it?'

My uncle was flabbergasted. He said, 'No, I cannot. I have to go to the temple,' and he brooded over his inescapable routine of prayer, meditation, dinner, and sleep.

'It's five o'clock now. Your work will take two hours—the paste must dry. We must give the paste its time to dry. But before I can take up your work, you see that man on your side, whose scalp is shining today but once upon a time who had a shock of hair like a coir doormat,' and he nodded in the direction of the bald man who was still waiting for a reply for the trustee. Jayraj continued his theme of the bald pate.

'About ten years ago one morning I noticed when he came to frame a calendar portrait of Brahma the Creator that he was growing thin on top; fortunately for us we cannot know the top of our own heads; and I did not tell him so that he might not feel discouraged about his matrimonial future; no one can question the why or wherefore of baldness; it is much like life and death. God gives us hair and takes it away when obviously it is needed elsewhere, that is all.'

Every word that Jayraj uttered pleased the bald man, who remarked at the end of it, 'Don't forget that I save on hair oil!' And he bowed his head to exhibit his shining top, at which I roared with laughter, Jayraj laughed out of courtesy, and my uncle smiled patronizingly, and into this pleasant and well-softened atmosphere the bald man pushed in a word about the business which had brought him there. 'The trustee . . .' he began, and Jayraj repeated, 'Oh, trustee, school trustee, temple trustee, hospital trustee, let him be anything; I have no use for trustees, and so why keep harping on them?'

The bald man sprang to his feet, approached the edge of the inner sanctum, leant forward almost in supplication and prayed, 'Please, please, don't send me back empty-handed; he will be upset, thinking that I have been loafing about.'

Now Jayraj looked properly concerned and said,

'He would think so, would he? All right, he shall have it even if I have to forgo sleep tonight. No more sleep, no more rest, until the trustee is pacified. That settles it.' He said finally, looking at my uncle. 'Yours immediately after the trustee's even if it means an all-night vigil.'

My uncle repeated, 'All night! I may not be able to stay long.'

'You don't have to,' said Jayraj. 'Please be gone, sir, and that is not going to affect my programme or promise. Trust me. You are determined to hang this young person's group picture on your wall tonight, perhaps the most auspicious date in your calendar! Yes, sir. Each unto himself is my philosophy. Tonight it shall be done. I usually charge three rupees for this size, Doctor; does it seem exorbitant to you?'

I felt startled when this man again addressed my uncle as 'Doctor'. My uncle considered the offer and said meekly, 'The print itself costs only two rupees.'

'In that case I will leave it to your sense of justice. Do you assume that frame and mount are in any sense inferior to the photo?'

Everyone on the bench looked concerned and nodded appreciatively at the progress of this dialogue (like the chorus in a Greek play) and my uncle said, 'All right, three.' He peeped out at the municipal clock tower. 'It is past five, you won't take it up before seven?'

Jayraj said, 'Not before eight.'

'I have to be going. How will it reach me?'

Jayraj said, 'I'll knock on your door tonight and deliver it. Maybe you could leave the charges, amounting to three rupees. Don't mistake me for asking for money in advance. You see that room.' He indicated an ante-chamber. 'It is full of pictures of gods, demons, and humans, framed in glass, ordered by people who never turned up again, and in those days I never knew how to ask for payment. If a picture is not claimed immediately I keep it for twenty years in that room. That's the law here. Anyway I don't want to keep your picture for twenty years. I will bring it to you tonight . . . or . . .' A sudden idea struck him. 'Why don't you leave this little fellow behind? He will collect the picture, and I will see that he comes home to you safely tonight.'

An impossible idea it seemed at first. My uncle shook his head and said, 'Oh, not possible. How can he stay here?'

'Trust me, have you no trust in me? Anyway at the end of the day I will deliver him and the photo at your door.'

'If you are coming our way, why do you want this boy to be left here?'

'To be frank, in order to make sure that I keep my promise and don't yield to any sudden impulse to shut my shop and run home.'

'Until midnight?'

'Oh, no, I was joking. Much earlier, much earlier.'

'What will he do for food? He is used to his supper at eight.'

Jayraj pointed to a restaurant across the street and said, 'I will nourish him properly. I love to have children around.'

My uncle looked at me and asked, 'Will you stay?'

I was thrilled. Jayraj was going to give me heavenly things to eat, and I could watch the procession of people and vehicles on Market Road. I pleaded, 'Uncle, don't be afraid.' I recollected all the dare-devilry of young men in the adventure stories I had heard. I wanted to have the pride of some achievement today. I pleaded with my uncle, 'Please leave me and go. I will come home later.'

Jayraj looked up and said, 'Don't worry about him,' and held out his hand. My uncle took out his purse and counted out three rupees on Jayraj's palm saying, 'I have never left him alone before.'

Jayraj said, 'Our boys must learn to get on by themselves. We must become a strong nation.'

*

After my uncle left, Jayraj pushed away my photo on to the floor and took in its place on the desk a group photo of the trustee's. He kept gazing on it and said, 'Not a very good photo. That Pictograph man again! So proud of his electronic flash! He claims he commands sunlight at his fingertips, but when he throws it on to the faces of a group before the camera, what do they do? They shut their eyes or open them wide as if they saw a ghost. For all the garland on his chest and all his pomposity, the man at the centre and all others in the group look to me like monkeys surprised on a mango tree . . .' The bald head kept swaying in approval. Jayraj constantly looked up from his work to make sure that the fellow was listening. I sat between them. Jayraj abruptly ordered, 'Child, move over, let that man come nearer.' I obeyed instantly.

This was my first day out, exciting and frightening at the same time. The world looked entirely different—the crowd at the market, which had seemed so entertaining before, was now terrifying. I feared that I might be engulfed and swept off, and never see my home again. As twilight came on and the street lamps were lit, I grew apprehensive. Somehow I felt I could not trust Jayraj. I stole a look at him. He looked forbidding. He wore a pair of glasses with thick lenses through which his eyeballs bulged, lending him a ghoulish look; he had an unshaven chin and grey mottled hair covering his forehead, khaki shirt and a blood-red dhoti, a frightening combination. All those smiles and friendly talk before my uncle was a show to entice me. He seemed to have his own sinister plans to deal with me once I was left at his mercy. He had become cold and aloof. Otherwise, why should he have asked me to yield my place to the bald man? The moment my uncle's back was turned this man's manner had changed; he looked grim and ignored me. Where was the nourishment he had promised? I was afraid to ask. I kept looking at the restaurant across the road in the hope that he might follow my gaze and take the hint, but his hands were sawing, hammering, pasting, and smoothing while his tongue wagged interruptedly. Having promised me nourishment, this man was not giving it a thought. Suppose I reminded him? But I lacked the courage to speak to him. With unappeased hunger on one side, my mind was also busy as to how to retrieve my photo from this horrible man and find my way home. I had not noticed the landmarks while coming. There were so many lanes ending on Market Road. I was not sure which one of them would lead me to Kabir Street, and from Kabir Street should I go up or down? A well stood right in the middle of that street, and beside it the striped wall of an abandoned temple in which the tailor was supposed to live. One went past it and came through onto Vinayak Street somehow. Vinayak Street seemed such a distant dream to me now. If some gracious god could put me down there,

at either end, I could always find my way home. I was
beginning to feel lost.

Jayraj paused for a moment to look at me and say,
'When I promise a time for delivery, I keep it.'
Analysing his statement, I found no hint of anything to
eat. 'When I promise a time ... etc.' What of the
promise of food? What did 'delivery' mean? Did it
include eating? It was a worrying situation for me. I
could not understand whether he implied that after
delivering his picture to the bald man he would
summon the restaurant-keeper and order a feast, or
did he simply mean that in due course he would nail
my photo on four sides with wood and glass and then
say, 'That is all, now get out.' When I tried to declare,
'I am very hungry, are you doing anything about it? A
promise is sacred and inescapable,' I found my voice
croaking, creaking, and the words in such a jumble and
mumble that it only attracted the other's attention and
conveyed nothing. He looked up and asked, 'Did you
speak?'

He looked fierce under the kerosene 'power-light'
hanging from the ceiling, and the huge shadow of its tin
reflector left half the shop in darkness. I had no doubt
that he enticed people in there, murdered them in cold
blood, and stored their bodies in the ante-room. I
remembered his mysterious references to the room,
and my uncle had understood. The wonder was that

Uncle should listen to all that and yet leave me behind. Of course, if it came to it, I could hit him with the little rod on the work bench and run away. This was a testing time, and Uncle perhaps wanted to try me out; hadn't they agreed that little boys should become tough? If he asked me in I should take care not to cross the threshold—but if he ordered food, but kept it as a bait far inside and then said, 'Come in here and eat'—perhaps then I should make a dash for the food, hit him with the steel rod, and run—tactics to be accomplished at lightning speed. Perhaps my uncle expected me to perform such deeds, and would admire my pluck. Hit Jayraj on the head and run and munch while running. While my mind was busy working out the details of my retreat, I noticed that the man had risen to his feet and was rummaging among old paper and cardboard, stacked in the back room. When he stood up he looked lanky and tall, with long legs and long limbs as if he had uncoiled himself. Rather snakelike, I thought.

For a moment I was seized with panic at the prospect of combating him. The bald man had edged closer and closer and had now actually stepped into the workshop, anticipating some excitement, the light from the power-lamp imparting a blinding lustre to his bald pate. Jayraj cried from the back room, 'Impossible to get at what one wants in this cursed place, must set apart a day for cleaning up ... Ah, here it is.' And he brought out a portrait in a grey mount, took it close to the light, and said, 'Come nearer, the print is rather faded.' They examined it with their heads abutting each other. I looked away. I realized that while they were brewing their nefarious plan I should remain alert but without giving them any sign of noticing. 'This is the man; at one time the richest doctor in Burma ...' I caught these words. Occasionally from time to time I turned my head just to look at them and caught them glancing at me and turning away. I too looked away, sharpening my ears not to miss a single word; somehow I was beginning to feel that their talk had something to do with me. Jayraj's loud and guffawing tone was all gone, he was now talking in a sinister undertone. 'Ten doctors employed under him. But this fellow was only a *chokra*; he sterilized needles and wrapped up powders and medicine bottles and cleansed the syringe; actually he must have started as this man's (tapping the photo) personal bootboy. When the Japanese bombed Rangoon, these people trekked back to our country, leaving behind their palatial home and several cars and everything, but still they managed to carry with them jewellery and much gold, and a bank account in Madras, and above all also a fifteen-day-old baby in arms. The doctor took ill and died on the way. There were rumours that he was pushed off a cliff by so-and-

so. The lady reached India half dead, lingered for a
year, and died. The baby was all right, so was the
chokra, all through the expedition. The *chokra*,
becoming all in all, took charge of all the cash and gold
and bank accounts after reaching this country,
impersonating the doctor. That poor woman, the
doctor's wife, need not have died, but this fellow kept
her a prisoner in the house and gave her some
injections and finished her. The cremation was a
double-quick affair across the river.'

The bald man now moved back to my side. Jayraj
had resumed his seat and was working on a frame. I
still kept looking away fixedly, feeling desperate at the
prospect before me—a total darkness had now fallen
on the city, and there was the hopelessness of getting
any refreshment.

They continued their talk in conspiratorial tones all
through. The bald man asked some question. Jayraj
replied, 'Who could say? I didn't know much about
them. I think that the fat woman must also have been
there all the time and a party to it. I learnt a lot from
a servant maid who brought this picture for framing
one day. I told her to call for it next day. She never
came. So far no sign of anyone claiming it.'

'The same fellow who sat here a little while ago!'
said the bald man in astonishment.

Jayraj lowered his voice and muttered, 'When I

called him "Doctor"—you must have seen his face!' and then they carried on their talk for a long while, which was all inaudible to me. I kept glancing at them and feeling their eyes on me all the time. Finally the tap-tap of the hammer ceased and he said, 'All right, this is finished. Let the glue dry a bit. Anyway it must be said to his credit: he tended the child and brought him up—only God knows the full truth.' He suddenly called me, held out to me the photograph salvaged from the dark chamber, and asked, 'Do you wish to take this home? I can give it to you free.' And they both stared at my face and the photo while he held it out. I had a momentary curiosity to look at the face of the man who had been the subject of their talk. The photo was very faded, I could glimpse only a moustache and little else; the man was in European clothes—if what they said was true, this was my father. I looked at their faces and noticed the sneering, leering expressions on them. I flung the photo back, got up without a word, and began to run.

*

I raced down Market Road, not aware of the direction I was taking. I heard the man shout after me, 'Come, come, I will frame yours and give it to you, and then take you home.' The bald man's squeaky voice added something to support his friend, but I ran. I bumped into people coming to the market and was cursed. 'Have you no eyes, these boys nowadays!' I feared Jayraj might shout, 'Catch him, don't let him get away.' Presently I slowed down my pace. I had no sense of direction but presently noticed Jagan's sweetmart on my right-hand side this time and knew that I was going back the way I had come. My head was drumming with Jayraj's speech. It was agonizing to picture my uncle cheating, murdering, and lying. The references to my father and mother touched me less; they were remote, unconvincing figures.

Blundering and groping along, I reached the end of Market Road. People looked at me curiously. I did not want to betray that this was my first outing alone, and so sauntered along, tried to look casual, whistled and hummed aloud, 'Raghupati Raghava Raja Ram.' The street lighting imperceptibly dimmed and grew sparser as I reached the foot of Lawley Statue. The Lawley Extension homes were tucked far back into their respective compounds, no way of knocking on their doors for any help; nor could I approach the boys leaning on their bicycles and chatting; they were senior boys who might make fun of me or beat me. A vagrant lay stretched full length on a side away from others; he looked wild and dreadful but he kept looking at me while others would not even notice my presence. I shrank away at the foot of this terrible statue, hoping that it would not suddenly start moving and march over me. The vagrant held out his hand and said, 'Give me a coin, I will buy something to eat.'

I turned my shirt pocket inside out to prove my statement. 'I have no money, not a paisa, and I am also hungry.'

'Go home then,' he ordered.

'I want to, but where is Vinayak Street?'

It was a grave risk betraying myself in this manner; if he realized that I was a lost soul he might abduct and sell me upcountry as a slave. 'I will go with you and show the way, will you tell your mother to give me a little rice for my trouble?'

Mother! Mother! My mind fell into a confusion . . . of that woman who died at Uncle's hand . . . I had all along felt my aunt was my mother. 'I have only an aunt, no mother,' I said.

'Aunts don't like me, and so go by yourself. Go back half the way you came, count three streets and turn on your left, if you know which is your left hand, and then turn right and you will be in Kabir Street . . .'

'Oh, I know Kabir Street, and the well,' I said with relief.

'Get onto it then, and take the turning beyond the well for Vinayak Street, don't wander all over the town like this. Boys like you must stay at home and read your lessons.'

'Yes, sir,' I said respectfully, feeling intimidated. 'Once I am back I promise to read my lessons.'

The directions that he gave helped me. I came through and found myself at the disused well in Kabir Street. When I reached Vinayak Street I felt triumphant. In that feeling of relief, even Jayraj's words ceased to rankle in my mind. The dogs in our street set up a stormy reception for me. At that hour the street was deserted, and the only guardians were the mongrels that roamed up and down in packs. They barked viciously at first but soon recognized me. Escorted by the friendly dogs, wagging their tails and wetting the lamp-posts in their delight at meeting me, I reached my house. My uncle and aunt were on the front doorstep and flung at me a jumble of inquiries. 'Your uncle wanted to start out again and look for you,' my aunt said.

Uncle lifted me practically half in the air in the sheer joy of our reunion, and asked, 'Where is the framer? He promised to leave you here. It is past ten o'clock now.'

Before I could answer my aunt said, 'I told you not to trust such persons.'

'Where is your photograph?'

I had not thought of an answer for that. What could I say? I only burst into tears and wept at the memory of all the confusion in my mind. Safer to weep than to speak. If I spoke I feared I might blunder into mentioning the other photo out of the darkroom.

My aunt immediately swept me in, remarking sorrowfully, 'Must be very, very hungry, poor child.' I sobbed, 'He didn't give me anything to eat.'

*

All night I lay tossing in my bed. I kicked my feet against the wall and groaned and woke up with a start from a medley of nightmares composed of the day's experience. My uncle was snoring peacefully in his room; I could see him through the open door. I sat up and watched him. He had impersonated a doctor, but it didn't seem to be a very serious charge, as I had always thought that all doctors with their rubber tubes and medical smell were play-acting all the time. Imprisoning and poisoning my mother—Mother? My aunt was my mother as far as I could see, and she was quite alive and sound. There wasn't even a faded photo of that mother as there was of my father. The photographer had said something about money and jewellery. I was indifferent to both. My uncle gave me all the money I needed, never refusing me anything at any time. Jewellery—those glittering pieces—one had better not bother about. You could not buy candy with gold, could you? To think that the refugees from

Rangoon should have carried such tinsel all the way! In my own way I was analysing and, examining the charges against my uncle, and found them flimsy, although the picture of him emanating out of dark whispers and furtive glances, in the background of a half-lit back room, was shocking.

I needed some clarifications very urgently. My aunt, sleeping on her mat at the edge of the open courtyard, stirred. I made sure that Uncle's snores were continuing, softly rose from my bed, and went over to her side. I sat on the edge of her mat and looked at her. She had observed my restlessness and asked, 'Why haven't you slept yet?'

I whispered, 'Aunt, are you awake? I want to tell you something.'

She encouraged me to speak. I gave her an account of Jayraj's narrative. She merely said, 'Forget it. Never mention it to your uncle.'

'Why?'

'Don't ask questions. Go back to your bed and sleep.'

I could do nothing more. I took the advice. The next day Jayraj managed to deliver the framed photo through someone who passed this way. My uncle examined it inch by inch by the light from the courtyard, and declared, 'Wonderful, good work, worth three rupees, surely.' He fumbled about with a hammer and nail looking for the right place, and hung it finally over his easy chair, right below the big portrait of his ancestor on the wall.

I acted on my aunt's advice and never asked any questions. As I grew up and met more people, I heard oblique references to my uncle here and there, but I ignored whatever I heard. Only once did I try to strangle a classmate at the college hostel in Madras who had gossiped about my uncle. Stirred by such information, sometimes I thought of him as a monster and I felt like pricking and deflating him the next time I met him. But when I saw him on the railway platform, waiting to receive me, the joy in his perspiring face moved me, and I never questioned him in any manner. After seeing me through the Albert Mission High School he had maintained me at a college in Madras; he wrote a postcard at least once a week, and celebrated my arrival during vacations with continuous feasting at home. He had probably gambled away a lot more money than he had spent on me. It didn't matter. Nothing ever mattered. He never denied me anything. Again and again I was prompted to ask the question, 'What am I worth? What about my parents?' but I rigorously suppressed it. Thus I maintained the delicate fabric of our relationship till the very end of his life. After his death, I examined his records—not a shade of correspondence or account to show any connection with Burma, except the lacquered casket with a dragon on it. He had bequeathed the house and all his possessions and a small annuity in the bank to me and left my aunt in my care.

AN AFTERNOON WITH
MR SAMPATH

[In this excerpt from the novel Mr Sampath, Srinivas,
the editor of the literary magazine the Banner, *sets
out to meet Sampath, the printer, who has recently
declared his inability to print the magazine because
his workers have gone on strike. What ensues is a
rather unusual encounter.]*

THE FOLLOWING DAYS proved dreary. Srinivas left
for his office punctually as usual every day. He took his
seat, went through the mail, and sat till the evening
making notes regarding the future of the *Banner*.
Sampath was hardly to be seen. The room below was
locked up and there was no sign of him.

Srinivas hardly had the heart to open his letters.
He could anticipate what they would contain. He did
not have a very large circle of readers; but the few that
read the paper were very enthusiastic. They complained:

'Dear Editor: It's a pity that you should be suspending the journal. Our weekend has become so blank without it.' He felt flattered and unhappy. His brother wrote from Talapur: 'I was quite taken aback to see your slip. Why've you suspended your journal indefinitely? Have you found it financially impossible? Is that likely to be the secret?' Srinivas felt indignant. Why did these people assume that a journal was bound to land itself in financial difficulties—as if that alone were the chief item? He indignantly wrote back a letter saying that financially it was all right, quite sound, and nobody need concern himself with it. He folded the letter and put it in an envelope. He put it away for posting, and went on to answer another letter and to say that the *Banner* would resume publication in a very short time; he wrote the same message to another and another. They piled up on one side of his untidy table. It was midday when he finished writing the letters. He looked at them again, one by one, as if revising, and told himself: 'What eyewash and falsehood! I'm not going to post these.' He tore up the letters and flung them into the wastepaper basket. His letter to his brother alone remained on the table. He went through it and was now assailed by doubts. He put it away and took out his accounts ledger. This was an aspect of the work to which he had paid the least attention. He now examined it page by page, and great uneasiness seized him. He picked up a sheet of paper and wrote on it: 'Mr Editor,' addressing himself, 'why are you deluding yourself? An account book cannot lie unless you are a big businessman and want to write it up for the benefit of the income-tax department. The *Banner*'s ledgers have no such grandeur about them. They are very plain and truthful. You have neglected the accounts completely. Your printer alone must be thanked for keeping you free from all worries regarding it. He was somehow providing the paper and printing off the sheets and dispatching copies. You received the money orders and disposed of the receipts in every eccentric way—sometimes paying the legitimate bills, more often paying off your rent and domestic bills. The printer has been too decent to demand his money, and so let it accumulate, taking it only when he was paid. I've a great suspicion that all his trouble with his staff was due to the *Banner*, it being almost the major work he did, and without getting any returns for it. If it is so, Mr Editor, your responsibility is very great in this affair. You have got to do something about it. I remain, yours truthfully, Srinivas.'

He folded it and put it in an envelope, pasted the flap, and wrote on it: 'To Mr Sampath, for favour of perusal.' He put the letter in his pocket and got up. He took his upper cloth from the nail on the wall, flung it over his shoulders and set out. He locked the room and went downstairs, his heart missing a beat at the sight of the bright brass lock on the front door of the press. He crossed Kabir Lane and entered the Market Road. It was midday and the sun was beating down fiercely. A few cars and buses drove along the road, stirring up the hot afternoon dust. The languor of the afternoon lay upon the place. Some of the shops in the market were closed, the owners having gone home for a nap. The fountain of the market square sparkled in the sun, rising in weak spurts; a few mongrels lay curled up at the market gate, a couple of women sat there with their baskets, a workman was sitting under a tree munching a handful of groundnuts he had bought from the women. Srinivas felt suddenly drowsy, catching the spirit of the hour himself. It was as if he were breathing in the free air of the town for the first time, for the first time opening his eyes to its atmosphere.

He suddenly realized what a lot he had missed in life and for so long, cooped up in that room. 'The death of a journal has compensations,' he reflected. 'For instance, how little did I know of life at this hour!' He toyed with the idea of going to the river for a plunge. 'I had nearly forgotten the existence of the river.' He hesitated, as he came before the National Stores. He would have to turn to his right here and cross into Ellaman Street if he were going to the river, but that would take him away from his destination, which was Sampath's house at New Extension.

He had two miles to go along the South Road. He felt suddenly very tired and his head throbbed faintly through the glare from the bleached roads; a couple of cars and lorries passed, stirring up a vast amount of dust, which hung like mist in the air. He saw a jutka coming in his direction, the horse limping along under the weight of the carriage. He called: 'Here, jutka, will you take me to Lawley Extension?' The jutka man, who had a red dhoti around his waist and a towel tied round his head, with nothing over his brown body, was almost asleep with the bamboo whip tucked under his arm. He started up at the call of 'Jutka!' and pulled the reins.

'Will you take me to Lawley Extension?' Srinivas repeated. He looked at Srinivas doubtfully. 'Oh, yes, Master. What will you give me?'

'Eight annas,' Srinivas said without conviction. Without a word the jutka man flicked the whip on the horse's haunch, and it moved forward. Srinivas watched it for a moment, and started walking down the South Road. The jutka driver halted his carriage, looked back and shouted: 'Will you give me fourteen annas?' Srinivas stared at him for a second, scorned to give him a reply and passed on. 'I would rather get burnt in the sun than have any transaction with these fellows,' he muttered to himself. A little later he heard once again the voice of the jutka man hailing him: 'Sir, will you give me at least twelve annas? Do you know how horse-gram is selling now?' Srinivas shouted back: 'I don't want to get into your jutka, even if you are going to carry me free,' and walked resolutely on. He felt indignant. 'The fellow would not even stop and haggle, but goes away and talks to me on second thoughts!' He felt surprised at his own indignation. 'There must be a touch of the sun in my head, I suppose. The poor fellow wants an anna or two more and I'm behaving like a——' His thoughts were interrupted by the rattling of carriage wheels behind him; he turned and saw the jutka pulling up close at his heels. The jutka driver, an unshaven ruffian, salaamed with one hand and said, rather hurt: 'You uttered a very big word, Master.' Srinivas was taken aback. 'I say, won't you leave me alone?' 'No, Master. I'm fifty years old and I have sat at the driver's seat ever since I can remember. You could give me the worst horse, and I could manage it.'

'That's all very well, but what has that to do with me?' Srinivas asked unhappily, and tried to proceed on his way. The jutka driver would not let him go. He cried ill-temperedly: 'What do you mean, sir, by going away?' Srinivas hesitated, not knowing what to do. 'Why is this man pestering me?' he reflected. The jutka driver insisted: 'What have you to say, Master? I've never been spoken to by a single fare in all my life—' And he patted his heart dramatically. 'And this will never know sleep or rest till it gets a good word from you again. You have said very harsh things about me, sir.' Srinivas wondered for a moment what he should do. It was getting late for him; this man would not let him go nor take him into his vehicle. The sun was relentless. He told the jutka driver: 'I'm a man of few words, and whatever I say once is final . . .'

'Sir, sir, please have pity on a poor man. The price of grass and horse-gram have gone up inhumanly.'

'I will give you ten annas.'

'Master's will,' said the jutka man, dusting the seat of the carriage. Srinivas heaved himself up and climbed in, the horse trotted along, and the wheels, iron bound, clattered on the granite. The carriage had its good old fragrance—of green grass, which was spread out on the floor, covered with a gunny sack for passengers to sit upon. The smell of the grass and the jutka brought back to his mind his boyhood at Talapur. His father occasionally let him ride with him in the jutka when he went to the district court. He sat beside their driver, who let him hold the reins or flourish the whip if there were no elders about, when the carriage returned home after dropping his father at the court. Some day it was going to be made quite a stylish affair with shining brass fittings and leather seats, but it remained, as far as he could remember, grass-spread, gunny-sack covered. The driver of that carriage used to be an equally rough-looking man called Muni, very much like the man who was driving now. Srinivas wondered whether it could be the same person. It seemed so long ago—centuries ago—yet it was as if here once again was the same person, his age arrested at a particular stage. Somehow the sight of the hirsute, rough-looking driver gave him a feeling of permanence and stability in life—the sort of sensation engendered by the sight of an old banyan tree or a rock. The smell of the grass filled him with a sudden homesickness for Talapur. He decided to make use of the present lull in activities to visit his ancient home. The driver went on repeating: 'The price of gram is—Master must have mercy on a poor man like me.'

At Lawley Extension the driver stopped his horse and grumbled at the prospect of having to go half a mile farther to New Extension. 'I clearly heard you say Lawley Extension, Master.' Srinivas edged towards the foothold. 'All right, then, I will get down and walk the rest of the distance.' The driver became panicky. He almost dragged him back to his seat, pleading: 'Master has a quick temper. Don't discredit me,' and whipped the horse forward. He went on to say: 'If only grass sold as it used to I would carry a person of your eminence for four annas ... as it is, I heard you distinctly say Lawley Extension. You had better tell me, sir, would anyone quote fourteen annas for New Extension? Please tell me, sir; you are a learned person, sir; please tell me yourself, sir ... Horse-gram—'

Sampath's house was at the Third Cross Road; he was standing at the gate of a small villa. Sampath let out a cry of welcome on seeing Srinivas and ran forward to meet him. Srinivas halted the jutka, paid him off briskly, and jumped out of the carriage. 'I was not certain of your door number, though I knew the road.' Broad roads and crossroads, fields of corn stretching away towards the west, and the trunk road bounding the east, with the bungalows of Lawley Extension beyond; one seemed able to see the blue sky for the first time here. 'What a lovely area!' Srinivas exclaimed.

'Yes, it looks all right, but if your business is in the town it is hell, I tell you. All your time is taken up in going to and fro.'

'What a fine bungalow!' Srinivas exclaimed.

'Yes, but I live in the backyard in an outhouse. The owner lives in this.'

He led him along a sidewalk to the backyard. On the edge of the compound there was an outhouse with a gabled front, a veranda screened with bamboo trellis, and two rooms. It was the printer's house. Srinivas felt rather disappointed at seeing him in his setting now, having always imagined that he lived in great style. The printer hurriedly cleared the veranda for his visitor; he rolled up a mat in great haste, kicked a roll of bedding out of sight, told some children playing there: 'Get in! Get in!' and dragged a chair hither and thither for Srinivas and a stool for himself. Srinivas noted a small table at the further end littered with children's books and slates; on the wall was a large portrait of a man with side whiskers, wearing a tattered felt hat, with a long pipe sticking out of a corner of his mouth. His face seemed familiar, and Srinivas was wondering where he might have met him. The printer followed his eyes and said: 'Do you recognize the portrait? Look at me closely.' Srinivas observed his face. 'Is that your picture?'

'Yes. You don't know perhaps that side of me. But I have not always been a printer. In fact, my heart has always been in make-up, costumes, and the stage—that was in those days. Lately I have not had much time for it. But even now no amateur drama is ever put on without me in it, and what a worry it is for me to squeeze in a little hour at the rehearsal, after shutting the printing office for the day.' He became reflective and morose at this thought, then abruptly sprang up and dashed inside and returned in a few minutes.

Srinivas guessed his mission indoors and said: 'I'm not in need of coffee now. Why do you worry your people at home?' The printer said: 'Oh! Is that so?' and addressed loudly someone inside the house: 'Here!

Our editor doesn't want you to be troubled for coffee; so don't bother.' He turned to Srinivas and said: 'Well, sir, I've conveyed your request. I hope you are satisfied.' Presently Srinivas heard footsteps in the hall; someone was trying to draw the attention of the printer from behind the door. The printer looked round with a grin and said: 'Eh? What do you say? I can't follow you if you are going to talk to me in those signals. Why don't you come out of hiding? Are you a *ghosha* woman?'

He giggled at the discomfiture of the other person at the door, and then got up and went over. A whispered conversation went on for a while and then the printer stepped out and said: 'Well, sir, my wife is not agreeable to your proposition. She insists upon your taking coffee as well as tiffin now. She has asked me how I can disgrace our family tradition by repeating what you said about coffee.' He looked at the door merrily and said: 'Kamala, meet our editor.' The person thus addressed took a long time in coming, and the printer urged: 'What is the matter with you, behaving like an orthodox old crony of seventy-five, dodging behind doors and going into purdah. Come on, come here, there is no harm in showing yourself.' Srinivas murmured: 'Oh, why do you trouble her?' and stepped forward in order to save the lady the trouble of coming out.

'This is my wife,' the printer said, and Srinivas

brought his hands together and saluted her. She returned it awkwardly, blushing and fidgety. She was a frail person of about thirty-five, neither good-looking nor bad-looking, very short, and wearing a saree of faded red, full of smoke and kitchen grime. She was nervously wiping her hands with the end of her saree, and Srinivas stood before her, not knowing what to say; an awkward silence reigned. The printer said: 'Very well, good woman, you may go now,' and his wife turned to go in with great relief, while Srinivas resumed his seat.

In a short while a tender voice called: 'Appa, Appa,' and the printer looked at the door and said: 'Come here, darling, what do you want?' A child, a girl of about four, came through, climbed on to his knee, approached him and whispered into his right ear. 'All right, bring the stuff down. Let us see how you are all going to serve this uncle,' pointing at Srinivas. The child went in with a smile, and came back with a tumbler of water and set it on the stool; it was followed by another child bringing another tumbler. The second child was slightly older. She complained: 'Look at Radhu; she will not let me carry anything.' The printer patted their backs and said: 'Hush! You must not fight. All of you try and bring one each.' He turned to Srinivas and said: 'Would you like to wash your hands?' Srinivas picked up the tumbler, went to the veranda steps and washed his hands, drying them on his handkerchief.

Now he found a sort of procession entering—a procession formed by four children, all daughters, ranging from nine to three, each carrying a plate or tumbler of something and setting it on a table and vying with each other in service. The small table was littered with plates. The printer dragged it into position before Srinivas and said: 'Well, honour me, sir—'

'What a worry for your wife, doing all this,' Srinivas said apologetically.

'She has got to do it in any case, sir. We've five children at home, and they constantly nag her—so this is no extra bother. Please don't worry yourself on that score.'

After the tiffin and coffee the printer cleared the table himself and came out bearing on his arm a small child under two years, who had not till then appeared.

'I'm very fond of this fellow, being my first son. I thought it would be so nice to hang up a sketch of this boy on the wall ...' he said. Anyway, we will have some entertainment now,' he continued. He called: 'Radhu!' and the young child came up. He said: 'Come on, darling, this uncle wants to see you dance. Call your sisters.' She looked happy at the prospect of a demonstration and called immediately: 'Sister! Chelli—' and a number of other names till all the four

gathered. She said: 'Father wants us to dance.' The
eldest looked shy and grumbled, at which their father
said: 'Come on, come on, don't be shy—fetch that
harmonium.' A harmonium was presently placed on his
lap. He pressed its bellow and the keys. The children
assembled on a mat and asked: 'What shall we do,
Father?' darting eager glances at their visitor. He
thought it over and said: 'Well, anything you like, that
thing about Krishna—' He pressed a couple of keys to
indicate the tune. The eldest said with a wry face: 'Oh,
that! We will do something else, Father.'

'All right, as you please. Sing that—' He suggested
another song. Another child said, 'Oh, Father, we will
do the Krishna one, Father.'

'All right.' And the printer pressed the keys of the
harmonium accordingly. There were protests and
counter-protests, and they stood arguing till the printer
lost his temper and cried arbitrarily: 'Will you do that
Krishna song or not?' And that settled it. His fingers
ran over the harmonium keys. Presently his voice
accompanied the tune with a song—a song of God
Krishna and the cowherds: all of them at their boyish
pranks, all of them the incarnation of a celestial group,
engaging themselves in a divine game. The children
sang and went round each other, and the words and
the tune created a pasture land with cows grazing
under a bright sun, the cowherds watching from a tree

branch and Krishna conjuring up a new vision for them with his magic flute. It seemed to Srinivas a profound enchantment provided by the father and the daughters. And their mother watched it unobtrusively from behind the door with great pride.

Srinivas was somehow a little saddened by the performance; there was something pathetic in the attempt to do anything in this drab, ill-fitting background. He felt tears very nearly coming to his eyes. Two more song-and-dance acts followed in the same strain. Srinivas felt an oppression in his chest, and began to wish that the performance would stop; the printer pumping the harmonium on his lap, the bundles of unwashed clothes pushed into a corner, and the children themselves clad uniformly in some cheap grey skirt and shirts and looking none too bright—it all seemed too sad for words. There was another song, describing the divine dance of Shiva: the printer's voice was at its loudest, and the thin voice of the children joined in a chorus.

Just at this moment someone appeared in the doorway and said: 'Master says he can't sleep. Wants you to stop the music.' An immediate silence fell upon the gathering. The printer looked confused for a moment and then said: 'H'm—seal up your master's doors and windows if he wants to sleep—don't come here for it. I'm not selling sleep here.' The servant turned and went away. Srinivas felt uncomfortable, wondering whether he were witnessing a very embarrassing scene. The printer turned to Srinivas: 'My landlord! Because he has given me this house he thinks he can order us about!' He laughed as if to cover the situation. He told the children: 'All right, you finish this dance, darlings.' He resumed his harmonium and singing, and the children followed it once again as if nothing had happened. It went on for another fifteen minutes, and then he put away the harmonium. 'Well, children, now go. Don't go and drink water now, immediately.' Srinivas felt some compliment was due to them and said: 'Who taught them all this?'

'Myself—I don't believe in leaving the children to professional hands.'

Srinivas addressed the children generally: 'You all do it wonderfully well. You must all do it again for me another day.' The children giggled and ran away, out of sight, and the printer's wife withdrew from behind the door. The printer put away the harmonium and sat back a little, sunk in thought. The children's voices could be heard nearly at the end of the street: they had all run out to play. The wife returned to the kitchen, and the evening sun threw a shaft of light through the bamboo trellis, chequering the opposite wall. A deep silence fell upon the company. Srinivas took the envelope he had brought out of his pocket and gave it to the printer, who glanced through it and said: 'It's my duty to see that the *Banner* is out again. Please wait. I will see that the journal is set up on a lino machine and printed off a rotary and dispatched in truck-loads every week. For this we need a lot of money. Don't you doubt it for a moment. I am going to make a lot of money, if it is only to move on to the main building and get that man down here to live as *my* tenant. And if ever I catch him playing the harmonium here, I will—I will—' He revelled in visions of revenge for a moment, and then said: 'A friend of mine is starting a film company and I'm joining him. Don't look so stunned: we shall be well on our way to the rotary when my first film is completed.'

'Film? Film?' Srinivas gasped. 'I never knew that you were connected with any film—'

'I've always been interested in films. Isn't it the fifth-largest industry in our country? How can I or anyone be indifferent to it? Come along, let us go, and see the studio.'

'Which studio? Where is it?'

'Beyond the river. They have taken five acres on lease.'

THE NAVARATRI ADVENTURE

[In the novel The Dark Room, *Savitri, the mother of three children, Kamala, Sumati and Babu, has a tough time running the household and dealing with the taunts of her uncaring husband Ramani. Over the Navaratri festivities the crisis in the household comes to a head and the spirit of the festival is lost in the unpleasantness.]*

IN THE MONTH of September, the streets rang with the cries of hawkers selling dolls—the earliest intimation of the coming Navaratri festival.

'Mother, aren't we buying some dolls this year for the festival?' asked Kamala.

'What's the use of buying them year after year; where are we to keep them?' Savitri replied.

'In the next house they have bought for ten rupees a pair of Rama and Sita, each image as large as a real child,' said Sumati.

'We have as many as we can manage. Why should we buy any more?' Savitri said.

'Mother, you must buy some new dolls,' Kamala and Sumati insisted.

'We have already three casks full of dolls and toys,' Savitri replied.

A day before the festival the casks were brought into the hall from an obscure storing-place in the house. Ranga, the servant, now had a lot of work to do. It was an agreeable change for him from the monotony of sweeping, washing clothes, and running errands. He enjoyed this work. He expressed his gay mood by tying a preposterous turban round his head with his towel and tucking up his dhoti.

'Oh, look at Ranga's turban!' screamed Kamala.

'Hey, you look like a cow,' added Sumati.

'Do I?' Ranga bellowed like a cow, and sent the children into fits of laughter.

'Don't waste time in playing. Open the casks and take out the dolls,' said Savitri.

Ranga untied the ropes and brought out the dolls in their yellowing newspaper wrappings. 'Handle them carefully, they may break.' In a short while dust and sheets of old newspaper, startled cockroaches and silverfish were all in a heap on one side of Ranga, and, on the other, were all the unwrapped dolls. Most of them had been given to Savitri by her mother, and the rest bought by her at various times. There they were—dolls, images, and toys of all colours, sizes, and shapes; soldiers, guards, and fat merchants; birds and beasts; gods and demons; fruits and cooking utensils; everything of clay, metal, wood, and cloth.

Ranga in his preposterous turban, stooping into the casks and bringing out the dolls, looked like an intoxicated conjurer giving a wild performance. The children waited, breathlessly watching for the next item, and shrieked at his absurd comments: 'Ah, here is my friend the parrot. He pecks at my flesh.' He would suck the blood on his finger and vow to break the parrot's beak before the end of the festival. He would hurriedly take out and put down a merchant or a grass-seller, complaining that they were uttering terrible swear-words and that he couldn't hold them. He would pretend to put the toy foods into his mouth and munch them with great satisfaction. Or he would scream at the sight of a cobra or a tiger. It was pure drama.

Savitri squatted down and wiped the dust off the dolls, and odd memories of her childhood stirred in her. Her eyes fell on a wooden rattle with the colour coming away in flakes, with which she had played when she was just a few months old. So her mother had told her. There was a toy flute into which she had wasted her babyhood breath. Savitri felt a sudden inexplicable self-pity at the thought of herself as an infant. She next felt an intense admiration for her mother, who never let even the slightest toy be lost but preserved everything carefully, and brought it all out for the Navaratri display. Savitri had a sudden longing to be back in her mother's house. She charged herself with neglecting her mother and not writing to her for several months now ... How frightfully she (Savitri) and her sister used to quarrel over these dolls and their arrangements! She remembered a particular Navaratri which was completely ruined because she and her sister had scratched each other's faces and were not on speaking terms. Poor girl! Who would have dreamt that she would grow into a bulky matron; with a doctor husband and seven children, away from everybody in Burma? That reminded her, she had not answered her letters received a month ago; positively, next Thursday she would write so as to catch the Friday steamer.

Now Ranga had put down a rosy-cheeked, auburn-haired doll which was eloquent with memories of her father. She remembered the evening when he had awakened her and given her the cardboard box containing this doll. How she adored this cardboard box and the doll and secretly used to thrust cooked rice into its mouth and steal sugar for it! Poor Father, so decrepit now! ...

A crash broke this reverie. Ranga had dropped a bluish elephant, as large as an ordinary cat.

'You ass, did you fall asleep?' she said sharply.

'Oh, it is broken!' wailed Sumati.

'Make him buy a new one, Mother. Don't give him his pay,' suggested Kamala.

Savitri felt very unhappy over the broken elephant: it was one of a pair that her mother had got from *her* mother, and it had been given to Savitri with special admonitions, and not to her sister, because she could not be depended upon to be so careful, and Savitri's mother had been very reluctant to separate the pair . . .

'I told you to be careful,' Savitri said, 'and yet, you ass—'

Ranga picked up the broken elephant. 'Oh, Madam, only its trunk is broken,' he announced gleefully.

'What is left of an elephant when its trunk is gone?' Savitri asked mournfully.

Ranga stood examining the trunkless elephant and said: 'It looks like a buffalo now. Why not have it in the show as a buffalo, Madam?'

'Fool, stop your jokes.'

'He doesn't care a bit!' Kamala said, horrified.

Ranga said to Kamala, 'Little madam, I know now how buffaloes are made.'

'How?' asked Kamala, suddenly interested.

'By breaking off the trunks of elephants,' said

Ranga. Then he said, 'Allow me to take this home, Madam.'

'Impossible,' said Kamala. 'Mother, don't let him take it. Tell him he must pay for it.'

'It is broken. Why do you want it?' Savitri asked.

'My little boy will tie a string round its neck, drag it about, and call it his dog. He has been worrying me to get him a dog for a long time.'

Kamala said, 'You won't get it,' and snatched the elephant from his hand.

Now all the dolls and toys were there, over five hundred of them, all in a jumble, like the creations of an eccentric god who had not yet created a world.

Babu had given definite instructions that the arrangement of the platform for the dolls was to be left entirely to him, and they were to do nothing till he returned from school. The girls were impatient. 'It is not a boy's business. This is entirely our affair. Why should we wait for him?'

Babu burst in at five o'clock and asked, looking about impatiently, 'Have you put up the platforms yet?'

'No, we are waiting for you. There is no hurry. Eat your tiffin and come,' said Savitri.

In two minutes he was ready to do his work. The girls jeered: 'Are you a girl to take a hand in the doll business? Go and play cricket. You are a man.'

'Shut up, or I will break all the dolls,' he said, at

which the girls screamed. Babu hectored Ranga and sent him spinning about on errands. With about eight narrow long planks, resting on raised supports at the ends, he constructed graduated step-like platforms. He pulled out of the rolls of bedding in the house all the white bedsheets and spread them on the planks; he disturbed all the objects in the house and confiscated all the kerosene tins and stools, etc. for constructing supports for the planks. He brought in bamboo poles and built a pavilion round the platform. He cut up strips of coloured paper and pasted them round the bamboo poles and covered their nakedness. He filled the whole pavilion with resplendent hangings and decorations. He did his work with concentration, while the two girls sat down and watched him, not daring to make the slightest comment; for at the slightest word Babu barked and menaced the speaker. He gave Ranga no time to regale the company with his jokes, but kept him standing on a high table in order to execute decorations on the pavilion roof.

In a couple of hours a gorgeous setting was ready for the dolls. Babu surveyed his work from a distance and said to his mother, 'You can arrange your knick-knacks now.' He turned to his sisters and said, 'Move carefully within the pavilion. If I find you up to some mischief, tearing the decorations or disturbing the platforms, you will drive me to a desperate act.'

Savitri said to the girls, pointing to the pavilion, 'Could you have made a thing like this? You prated so much when he began the work.' Sumati was a little apologetic and appreciative, but Kamala said, 'If you had given me a little paste and paper I too could have done it. It is not a great feat.' Savitri said, 'Now lift the dolls carefully and arrange them one by one. Sumati, since you are taller than Kamala you will arrange the dolls on the first four platforms, and, Kamala, you will do it on the lower four platforms. Don't break anything, and don't fight.'

In an hour a fantastic world was raised: a world inhabited by all God's creations that the human mind had counted; creatures in all gay colours and absurd proportions and grotesque companies. There were green parrots which stood taller than the elephants beside them; there were horses of yellow and white and green colours dwarfed beside painted brinjals; there was a finger-sized Turkish soldier with not a bit of equipment missing; the fat, round-bellied merchant, wearing a coat on his bare body, squatted there, a picture of contentment, gazing at his cereals before him, unmindful of the company of a curly-tailed dog of porcelain on one side and a grimacing tiger on the other. Here and there out of the company of animals and vegetables and mortals emerged the gods—the great indigo-blue Rama, holding his mighty bow in one hand, and with his spouse Sita by his side, their serenity unaffected by the company about them, consisting of a lacquered wooden spoon, a very tiny celluloid doll clothed in a pink saree, a sly fox with a stolen goose in its mouth, and a balancing acrobat in leaf-green breeches; there stood the great Krishna trampling to death the demon serpent Kalinga, undistracted by the leer of a teddy bear which could beat a drum. Mortals and immortals, animals and vegetables, gods and sly foxes, acrobats and bears, warriors and cooking utensils, were all the same here, in this fantastic universe conjured out of coloured paper, wood, and doll-maker's clay.

'It is all very well now, but the trouble will be in putting them all back in their casks carefully after nine days. It is the most tedious work one could think of,' said Savitri.

'Mother, don't dismantle them again. Why can't we let them stay out for ever? It is always so terribly dull when the decorations are torn down and the dolls are returned to the casks.'

Next morning Babu took a look at his work and decided to improve it. It was all very well as far as gum and paper could go, but the lighting was defective. All the illumination that the pavilion got was from the bulb hanging a few yards from it in the hall. He would get his friend Chandru in, and fix up a festoon of ornamental coloured bulbs under the pavilion arch; he would transform the doll pavilion into something unique in the whole of the Extension.

He brought Chandru in the afternoon. Chandru was very much his senior, but Babu spent much of his time with him. Chandru was studying in the Intermediate and had a genius for electricity. He had made miniature dynamos, electric bells, and telegraph sets.

Sumati and Kamala were delighted. 'It is going to beat the pavilion in the police inspector's house,' they said ecstatically. Chandru worked wonders with a piece of wire and a spanner. In a short while he had created a new circuit with an independent switch. When the switch was put on, a festoon of coloured bulbs twinkled in the archway and two powerful bulbs flooded all the dolls with a bluish light.

'When you turn the switch on in the evening, do it very carefully,' warned Chandru, and left.

It was a great triumph for Babu. He felt very proud of being responsible for the illumination. 'If you like I will ask him to come and add an electric train to the dolls. That will be wonderful,' he said.

At five o'clock the two girls worried Babu to put the lights on. He told them he knew the right time to do it and warned them not to go near the switch. 'Lighting at six,' he said.

'We will be out at six,' they protested, 'inviting

people. A lot of our friends will be coming now to invite us to their houses, and we would so love to have the illuminations at once. Please.'

'Will you leave that to me or not? I know when to do it, and I want you to mind your own business now.'

Savitri said to Babu, 'Don't be so strict. You have done everything for their sake, why should you grudge them the lights now?'

'All right, at five-thirty,' said Babu.

At five-thirty nearly a dozen visitors had already arrived. Everyone wore bright silks, and sat gazing at the dolls. Finding so many ladies sitting in the hall, Babu hesitated at the door, wondering how he was to reach the switch in the pavilion. He called Sumati and said, 'With the tip of your finger push that small rod to one side, to the left. You must do it very gently.'

Sumati pushed the switch gently, then less gently, and then Babu shed his shyness and dashed to the switch. He rattled it but nothing happened. Not only were the pavilion lights not on, but the usual hall bulbs had also gone out. Babu looked at Sumati and said, 'I knew that if I let you touch it something or the other would happen.' He stood contemplating the new circuit, rattled the switch once more and said that somebody had tampered with it and that he would get at that person soon. Muttering that one couldn't plumb the depth of mischief in girls, he walked out of the hall.

Nobody yet realized that anything was wrong because there was good sunlight.

At about seven-thirty the conditions were different. There was no light in the house. Visitors were received in the pale light of a hurricane lantern, and the pavilion was lit by flickering oil-lamps transferred from the puja room. The atmosphere was dim and gloomy. The sisters' rage knew no limits. 'Mother, do you understand now why we did not want any boy to come and interfere in our business? As if it wouldn't have been a pretty sight without those lights. Who wanted them anyway? We never asked him to come and fix the lights.'

Babu was in utter despair. Chandru had gone to the cinema and would not be back till nearly ten. And he had no friend who knew anything about electricity.

'Send someone to the electric office,' said Savitri.

'Shall I go?' asked Babu.

Savitri hesitated. How could she send him out all alone so late? 'Take Ranga with you.'

And protected by Ranga's company, Babu set out to the electric office in Market Road—a distance of about two miles.

Babu stood before the entrance to the electric office and said to someone, 'There is no light in our house in the South Extension.'

'Go in and tell it to the people you will find there.'

Babu went in and was directed to a room in which three fellows were sitting, smoking and talking. One of them asked him, 'Who are you, boy?'

'The lights are out in our house in the South Extension.'

'Put the switches on,' somebody said, and all three laughed.

Babu felt awkward, but the lights had to be set right. He pleaded: 'Can't you do something? We have tried the switches.'

'Probably the fuse has gone. Have you seen if the meter fuses are all right?'

'I haven't. There is nobody in the house.'

'Then, why do you want the lights? If the meter fuse is burnt, it is none of our concern. We will come only when the pole fuse is burnt. Go and see if the meter fuse is all right.'

When Babu reached home he found his father had already arrived. He was in a terrible temper. Ranga's absence had delayed the opening of the garage door and had infuriated him. In that state he had entered the house and found it dark. Now failure of electric current was one of the things which completely upset him. He stood in the doorway and roared, 'What is this?' Savitri let the question wither without an answer. The girls did not dare to answer.

'Is everybody in this house dead?' he asked.

Savitri was angered by this, 'What a thing to say on a day like this, and at this hour! I have seen very few who will swear and curse at auspicious times as you do.'

'Then why couldn't you have opened your precious mouth and said what the matter was?'

'There is nothing the matter. You see that there is no current and that there are no lights, and that's all that's the matter.'

'Has anybody gone to the electric office?'

'Babu has gone there.'

'Babu, Babu, a very big man to go.'

This irrational pointless cynicism enraged Savitri, but she remained silent.

Ramani passed in to undress, grumbling all the way. Standing in the dark, he cursed the whole household and all humanity. 'Ranga! Here, Ranga!' he howled in the dark.

'I told you Ranga had gone to the electric office with Babu,' Savitri said.

'Why should everybody go to the electric office? Is Babu to be protected like a girl? Whose arrangement is it?' he raved. 'Bring some light, somebody.'

Savitri sent the hurricane lantern along with Kamala. Kamala set the lamp on the floor while her father looked at her fixedly. 'Here, that's not the place to put the lantern. Do I want illumination for my feet? Bad training, rotten training.' He lifted the lantern and looked about for a place and said, 'Don't you know that when you bring a lantern you have to bring a piece of paper to keep under it? When will you learn all this?

'Very well, Father,' Kamala said, much intimidated by his manner.

This submissiveness pleased Ramani. He said, 'You must be a good girl, otherwise people won't like you.' He placed the lantern on the window sill. Kamala turned to go and took a few steps. 'Little girl, don't shuffle your feet while walking,' said Ramani.

'Hereafter I will walk properly, Father.'

He was thoroughly pleased with her. He felt he ought to bestow on her some attention—honour her with a little conversation. 'Have you been in the dark all the evening?'

'No, Father, we had current till six o'clock and then—' She hesitated.

'What happened?'

'Babu's friend put up new bulbs for the dolls, and when Babu pressed a switch something happened, and all the lights went out.'

When Babu returned from the electric office he found his father standing in the hall and shouting. As soon as he sighted Babu he asked, 'You blackguard, who asked you to tamper with the electric lights?'

Babu stood stunned. 'Don't try to escape by being silent. Are you following your mother's example?'

'No, Father.'

'Who asked you to tamper with the electric lights?'

'I didn't touch anything. I brought in Chandru. He knows all about electricity.'

His father moved towards him and twisted his ear, saying, 'How often have I asked you to keep to your books and mind your business?'

'I'll try to set it right, Father, as soon as Chandru comes home.'

'Who asked you to go near the dolls' business? Are you a girl? Tell me, are you a girl?'

This insistent question was accompanied by violent twists of the ear. Babu's body shook under the grip of his father's hot fingers. 'No, Father, I am not a woman.'

'Then why did you go near the dolls?' He twisted the other ear too. 'Will you do a thing like this again? Tell me!'

In helpless anger Babu remained silent. His father slapped him on the cheek. 'Don't beat me, Father,' he said, and Ramani gave him a few more slaps. At this point Savitri dashed forward to protect Babu. She took him aside, glaring at her husband, who said, 'Leave him alone, he doesn't need your petting.' She felt faint with anger. 'Why do you beat him?' was all that she could ask, and then she burst out crying. At the sight of her tears, Babu could not control himself any longer. He sobbed, 'I didn't know . . . I didn't know it was wrong to add those lights.'

Ramani left, remarking that he was sick of this sentimental show. He came back after a wash. 'Now to dinner. We will manage with the available lights.' Savitri squatted down, her face covered with her hands. 'I see that you are holding a stage-show. I can't stand here and watch you. Are you coming in for food or not? . . . All right, you can please yourself.' He turned and walked to the dining-room calling, 'Has that effeminate boy eaten? Babu, come for your dinner!'

When he was gone, Savitri rose, went to the dark room next to the store, and threw herself on the floor. Later the cook tracked her down there and requested her to take her food, but she refused. The children came to her one by one and tried to coax her. She turned her face to the wall and shut her eyes.

LEELA AND THE HEADMASTER

[In Narayan's semi-autobiographical novel The English Teacher, *the teacher Krishna's wife Susila passes away after a sudden illness, leaving their daughter Leela in his care. The episode that follows traces the wonderful bond between father and daughter, and recounts Leela's first days in a school that is unlike any other.]*

THE OLD WOMAN was saying: 'A man must marry within fifteen days of losing his wife. Otherwise he will be ruined. I was the fourth wife to my husband and he always married within three weeks. All the fourteen children are happy. What is wrong?' she asked in an argumentative manner. The bus roared and started and jerked forward. My daughter sat in my arms, watching the whole scene spellbound. As the bus moved my mother said: 'Don't fail to give her an oil anointment and bath every Friday. Otherwise she will lose all her hair ...'

I was never a sound sleeper at any time in life, but now more than ever I lay awake most of the night, sleeping by fits and starts. My mind kept buzzing with thoughts and memories. In the darkness I often felt an echo of her voice and speech or sometimes her moaning and delirious talk in sickbed. The child lay next to me sleeping soundly. We both slept in my little study on the front veranda. The door of the room in which my wife passed away remained shut. It was opened once a week for sweeping, and then closed again and locked. This had been going on for months now. It was expected that I should leave the house and move to another. It seemed at first a most natural and inevitable thing to do. But after the initial shock had worn out, it seemed unnecessary and then impossible. At first I put it down to a general disinclination for change and shifting. To remove that chair, and that chaotic table with its contents ... and then another and another ... We had created a few favourite corners in the house, and it seemed impossible to change and settle in a new house. My daughter had played on the edge of that veranda ever since she came to me as a seven-month baby. Yes, at first I put it down to a general disinclination for change, but gradually I recalled the experience of life in that house was too precious and that I wouldn't exchange it for anything. There were subtle links with a happy past;

they were not merely links but blood channels, which fed the stuff of memory ... Even sad and harrowing memories were cherished by me; for in the contemplation of those sad scenes and hapless hours, I seemed to acquire a new peace, a new outlook; a view of life with a place for everything.

The room which was kept shut had an irresistible fascination for my daughter. She looked at the door with a great deal of puzzlement. On that unhappy day when we had returned from the cremation ground, the child had also just come home. 'Father, why is that door shut?' It threw us into a frenzy. We did not know what to reply. The house at that time was full of guests, all adults—all looking on, suffering, and bewildered by death. Death was puzzling enough, but this question we felt was a maddening conundrum. We looked at each other and stood speechless. My daughter would not allow us to rest there. She repeated authoritatively: 'Why is that door closed?' My father-in-law was deeply moved by this. He tried to change her mind by asking: 'Would you like to have a nice celluloid doll?'

'Yes, where is it?' she asked.

'In the shop. Let us go and buy one.' She picked up her green coat, which she had just discarded, and said: 'All right, let us go, Grandfather.' It had been a strenuous morning and we had eaten our food late in the day and were about to rest. He looked forlorn. 'Come on,' she said, and he looked at me pathetically. I told my daughter, 'You are a good girl, let your grandfather rest for a little while and then he will take you out . . .' She said: 'Why have you had your meal so late?' Another inconvenient question under which we cringed. We were all too fatigued to invent new answers to beguile her mind. She waited for a moment and returned to her original charge. 'Doll—come on Grandfather.' He had by this time thrown himself on the floor and was half sunk in sleep. I said: 'Child, you are a nice child. Allow your grandfather to rest. He will take you out and buy two dolls.' She was displeased at this, removed her coat and flung it down. I couldn't check her, as I would have done at other times. She looked at me fixedly and asked: 'Why is that door closed?' At which everyone was once again convulsed and confused and dismayed. She seemed to look on this with a lot of secret pleasure. She waited for an answer with ruthless determination. 'Mother is being given a bath, that is why the door is closed . . .' She accepted the explanation with a nod of her head, and then went up to her wooden trunk containing toys, rummaged and picked out a rag book. I went away to my room and reclined on my easy chair. As I closed my eyes, I heard her footfalls approaching. She thrust the rag book under my nose and demanded: 'Read this story.' I had read that 'story' two hundred times already. The book was dirty with handling. And she always kept it with all the junk in her trunk. It had illustrations in green, and a running commentary of a couple of lines under each. It was really not a story, there was not one in it, but a series of illustrations of a tiger, a lion, an apple, and Sam—each nothing to do with the other. But Leela would never accept the fact that they were disconnected. She maintained that the whole book was one story—and always commanded me to read it; so I fused them all into a whole and gave her a 'story'—'Sam ate the apple, but the lion and the tiger wanted some of it . . .' and so on. And she always listened with interest, completely accepting the version. But unfortunately I never repeated the same version and always mystified her! 'No, Father, Sam didn't hit the tiger,' she would correct. So when this book was pressed into my hand today my heart parched at the thought of having to narrate a story . . . 'Once upon a time . . .' I said, and somehow went on animating the pictures in the book with my narration. She said: 'You are wrong, Father, it didn't happen that way. Your story is very wrong . . .'

Towards the evening she came up once again and asked: 'The door is still closed, Father. Is she bathing still?'

'H'm. If the door is open, she may catch a cold . . .'

'Don't you have to go to her?'

'No . . .'

'Is she all alone?'

'There is a nurse who looks after her.'

'What is a nurse?'

'A person who tends sick people.'

'You don't have to go and stay with Mother any more, ever?'

'No, I will always be with you.' She let out a yell of joy and threw herself on me.

Four days later, she stole into my room one evening, and whispered, with hardly suppressed glee: 'Father, say what I have done?'

'What is it?'

'There was no one there and it wasn't locked; so I pushed the door open and went in. Mother is not there!' She shook with suppressed glee, at the thought of her own escapade.

'God, give me a sensible answer for this child,' I prayed.

'Oh,' I said casually and added, 'the nurse must have taken her away to the hospital.'

'When will she be back?'

'As soon as she is all right again,' I replied.

The first thing that woke me in the morning was the cold hands of my daughter placed on my forehead and the shout 'Appa', or sometimes she just sat, with her elbows on the ground and her chin between her palms, gazing into my face as I lay asleep. Whenever I opened my eyes in the morning, I saw her face close to mine, and her eyes scrutinizing my face. I do not know what she found so fascinating there. Her eyes looked like a pair of dark butterflies dancing with independent life, at such close quarters.

'Oh, Father has woken up!' she cried happily. I looked at her with suspicion and asked: 'What have you been trying to do so close to me?'

'I only wanted to watch, that is all. I didn't wake you up.'

'Watch what?'

'I wanted to watch if any ant or fly was going to get into you through your nose, that is all . . .'

'Did any get in?'

'No. Because I was watching.' There was a hint in her tone as if a sentry had mounted guard against a formidable enemy.

'What do you do when you sleep, Father?' Once again a question that could not be answered by an adult; perhaps only another child could find an answer for it. 'I was saying something close to you and yet you didn't reply.'

'What were you saying?'

'I said: "There is a peppermint, open your mouth!" '

After these preambles we left the bed. I rolled her

about a little on the mattress and then she sat up and picked a book from my table and commanded: 'Read this story.' I had no story book on my table. She usually picked up some heavy critical work and brought it to me. When I put it back on the table, she brought out her usual catalogue of the Calcutta mail order firm, and asked me to read out of it. This happened almost every morning. I had to put away the book gently and say to her: 'Not now. We must first wash.'

'Why?'

'That is how it must be done.'

'No. We must first read stories,' she corrected me.

'We must first wash, and then read stories,' I persisted.

'Why?'

'Because it is Goddess Saraswati and we must never touch her without washing.'

'What will she do if we touch her without washing?'

'She will be very unhappy, and she is the goddess of learning, you see, and if you please her by washing and being clean, she will make you very learned.'

'Why should I be learned?'

'You can read a lot of stories yourself without my help.'

'Oh! What will you do then?' she asked, as if pitying a man who would lose his only employment in life.

It was as a matter of fact my chief occupation in life. I cared for little else. I felt a thrill of pride whenever I had to look after the child and work for her. It seemed a noble and exciting occupation—the sole responsibility for a growing creature.

*

Nowadays I went about my work with a light heart. I felt as if a dead load had been lifted. The day seemed full of possibilities of surprise and joy. At home I devoted myself to my studies more energetically. The sense of futility was leaving me. I attended to my work earnestly. All the morning I sat preparing my day's lectures. My little daughter watched me curiously. 'Father is reading!' she exclaimed. She drew a chair close to mine and sat up with a book, with any book that caught her fancy, till she saw a squirrel or a sparrow alighting on the roof of the opposite house, and exclaimed: 'Father, the sparrow has come. Do they also read? Do they also go to school?'

'Little girl, just go out near the gate and ask,' I said, with the idea of getting on with my work. Once she had gone out, she slowly got interested in something or the other and forgot to come back. When she mentioned school one morning, I pricked up my ears. When I returned home that same evening, the child was out. There was only the old lady in the kitchen. I asked: 'Where is Leela?'

'Oh, she has gone to the school,' the old lady replied.

'Which school?' I asked with feigned ignorance.

'That baby's school, in the next street. I took her there once or twice in the afternoon, because she liked to see the other children, and they all like her very much there. Today the teacher said he would bring her back in the evening. She wouldn't come away either: because she is making some animals and other things with clay. They have also given her scissors and coloured paper to cut. She is so happy!'

'Why didn't you tell me before that you had taken her there?'

'I took her out on two days just for a few minutes. When the child in the next house came home in the afternoon and went back to school, Leela also went with her one day,' she said and added, 'poor thing, it was some way of engaging her mind and keeping her from longing for her mother!'

The child came home half-an-hour later. Her teacher left her at the gate and went away. 'Father,' she screamed at the gate, 'I've been to school like you.' I went out and picked her up in my arms. The teacher had moved off a few yards.

'Is that your teacher?' I asked.

'Yes.'

'Call him,' I said. At which she shouted: 'Schoolmaster!' and the teacher turned back. 'Come back and speak to my father.'

'You are the headmaster of the school?' I asked.

'Yes.'

'Is there any class to which this girl can be admitted?'

'Oh, yes. She will be happy. We shall be very glad to admit her.'

'Any long hours?' I asked.

'Oh, no, she can come any time and go away when she likes. No restrictions. Please send her. She will be happy with us.'

'May I know your name?'

'Just "headmaster" will do . . .' he said.

The child was dancing with joy. She was full of descriptions of her school. 'Father, do you know I have made a clay brinjal? The teacher said it was nice.'

'All right, all right,' I said, and sat by her side and made her take some tiffin which the old lady had prepared. She was too excited to relish anything. I coaxed her to eat. And then took her to the bathroom. Her face was streaked with the clay she had been handling. I soaked a towel in water and rubbed her cheeks till they glowed. And then I sent her in to the old lady and had her hair combed.

I took her out on her usual walk. I took her

through the busy thoroughfare of Market Road. She loved the bustle of Market Road and kept asking questions and I found her view of life enchanting. I bought her some sweets at the stores. She mainly talked about her school. 'Father, at our school, I have a friend. You know her father gives her lots of sweets every day. Why do you always give me only one or two?'

'Children must not eat more than two at a time,' I replied.

'She is a good girl, always plays with me at school,' the child said. 'Shall I also grow tall when I go to school?'

'Yes, certainly.'

'Why do you go to that far-off school, and not to our school, Father?' she said. She saw some villagers moving about with turbans on their heads. She asked: 'Do they wear those things on their heads, even when they sleep?' I don't know what idea crossed her mind at such times. I took her to the river bank. She ran about on the sand. She watched the other children playing. She whispered: 'That girl is in our school.'

'What is her name?'

'Kamala,' she said.

'Is she your friend?'

'She is a very good girl.'

'Go and play with her if you like.' The girl was

playing with another group around a circle on the sand. At my suggestion Leela blinked and said with great seriousness: 'She will be very angry if I ask to be taken also.'

'Call her, let me see,' I said.

'Kamala, Kamala,' she called faintly, and then added: 'That is her school name, she doesn't like to be called so when she is not in school.' We passed on. She stood near other girls also and pointed them out to me as her school friends, but she would not go near anyone or call aloud. She seemed to identify her friends in a general way, whatever might be their names and their schools; as far as she was concerned they were all her friends and schoolmates. She was endowing each of them with any character she chose.

Next morning there was great activity. She was to be put to school. I was as excited as if I myself were to be put to school. I did little work at my table that day. I ran about the house in great excitement. I opened her trunk and picked out a shirt and skirt, fresh ones, printed cotton. When she saw them my daughter put them back and insisted upon wearing something in lace and silk. 'Baby, you must not go to school wearing laced clothes. Have you ever seen me going with any lace on?'

'It's because you have no lace skirts, that is all,' she said. 'No, Father, I want that for school. Otherwise they will not allow me in.' She threw her clothes about and picked up a deep green shirt, with a resplendent lace three inches wide, and a red skirt studded with stars: the whole thing was too gorgeous for a school. Her mother had selected them for her on a birthday, at the Bombay Cloth Emporium. Two evenings before the birthday we had gone there, and after an hour's search she had picked up these bits for the child, who was delighted with the selection. I protested against it and was told, 'Gaudy! There is nothing gaudy where children are concerned, particularly if they are girls. Whom are these for if they are not meant to be worn by children?'

'Go on, go on,' I said cynically. 'Buy yourself two of the same pattern if you are so fond of it.' But the cynicism was lost on her. She disarmed me by taking it literally and said: 'No, no. I don't think they weave sarees of this pattern? Do they?' she asked turning to the shopman.

The child was excessively fond of this piece and on every occasion attempted to wear it. Today she was so adamant that I had to yield to her. She tried to wear them immediately, but I said: 'After your hair is combed and you have bathed . . .' And now as I put her clothes back in the box she grew very impatient and demanded: 'Bathe me, Father, bathe me, Father.' I turned her over to the old lady's care and arranged the box, carefully folded and kept away her clothes. She had over forty skirts and shirts. Her mother believed in stitching clothes for her whenever she had no other work to do, and all the child's grandparents and uncles and aunts constantly sent her silk pieces and clothes ever since the day she was born. The result was she had accumulated an unmanageable quantity of costly clothes, and it was one of my important occupations in life to keep count of them.

She was ready, dressed in regalia, and stood before me, a miniature version of her mother. 'Let us go,' she said, and for a moment I was unaware of whether the mother or the daughter was speaking—the turn of the head and lips!

'I must carry books,' she insisted.

'No, no, not today . . .'

'My teacher will be angry if I don't take my books,' she said, and picked up her usual catalogue. She clasped it to her little bosom, and walked out with me, bubbling with anticipation and joy. The school was in the next street. A small compound and a few trees around a small brick-red building. The noise those children made reached me as I turned the street. The headmaster received us at the gate. As soon as we entered the gate, a few other children surrounded Leela and took her away. She left me without a thought. She behaved as if she had been in that school for years and years.

The headmaster was in raptures over the new arrival. He said: 'Won't you come and have a look round?'

He had partitioned the main hall into a number of rooms. The partition screens could all be seen, filled with glittering alphabets and pictures drawn by children—a look at it seemed to explain the created universe. You could find everything you wanted—men, trees, animals, skies and rivers. 'All these—work of our children . . .' he explained proudly. 'Wonderful creatures! It is wonderful how much they can see and do! I tell you, sir, live in their midst and you will want nothing else in life.' He took me round. In that narrow space he had crammed every conceivable plaything for children, see-saws, swings, sand heaps and ladders. 'These are the classrooms,' he said. 'Not for them. For us elders to learn. Just watch them for a while.' They were digging into the sand, running up the ladder, swinging, sliding down slopes—all so happy. 'This is the meaning of the word joy—in its purest sense. We can learn a great deal watching them and playing with them. When we are qualified we can enter their life . . .' he said. The place was dotted with the coloured dresses of these children, bundles of joy and play. 'When I watch them, I get a glimpse of some purpose in existence and creation.' He struck me as an extraordinary man.

'If they are always playing when do they study?'

'Just as they play—I gather them together and talk to them and take them in and show them writing on boards. They learn more that way. Everybody speaks of studies through games but nobody really practises it. It becomes more the subject of a paper in some pompous conference and brings a title or preference to the educational administrator. Oh, don't allow me to speak too much on this subject as you will find me a terrible bore . . .' He was a slight man who looked scraggy; evidently he didn't care for himself sufficiently. His hair fell on his nape, not because he wanted it to grow that way, but, I was sure, because he neglected to get it cut. His coat was frayed and unpressed. I liked him immensely. I was sure there were many things about him which would fascinate me. I was seized with a desire to know more of him. I asked him: 'Please visit me some day.'

*

Sunday. I decided to spend the entire day in the company of the child. Of late my college work and the extra activities took up so much of my time that I spent less than two hours a day with the child. It was a painful realization. 'Oh God,' went up my prayer, 'save me from becoming too absorbed in anything to look after the child properly.' And I felt very sorry and guilty when I returned home at nights and found the child asleep.

She had her own plans for the day. As soon as she got up and was ready for the road, she insisted upon being taken to the school.

'This is Sunday, you don't have to go,' I pleaded.

But it was no use. 'You don't know about our school. We have school.' She put on her coat and stepped out. I went out with her. 'Why do you follow me, Father?' she asked.

'I too want to see your school today,' I said.

'But my friends are filled with fear if they see you. Don't come with me, Father,' she pleaded.

'No, I will take good care not to frighten them,' I assured her. She stood for a moment undecided, looking at me and said to herself: 'Poor Father, let him come too,' and smiled patronizingly.

There was no sign at the school to show that it was a Sunday. It was alive with the shouts of children—about twenty of them had already gathered and were running about and playing: the swings and see-saw were all in full use. The headmaster was with them.

'You don't rest even on a Sunday?' I asked the headmaster.

'Rest? This is all right for a rest, what else should I do? They just come in, play, throw the sand about, and go away, and we also do it with them. It is quite good, you know. I feel quite happy. What else should I do on a Sunday?'

'Something to differentiate it from other days ...'

'Quite. We don't do sums today. We just sing, hear stories, and play ...' His eyes were red. He coughed. He did not look as if he had had sleep at night.

'What is the matter with you?' I could not help asking.

'I suffer from sleeplessness, my friend,' he said. 'It is some years since I had anything like sleep. I sleep about an hour. I used to make myself very miserable about it at first. But now I am used to it. I make up stories for children and I hardly feel the time passing. Come in and see.' He took me into his room. It was thatch-roofed. Its floor was covered with clay, and the walls were of bamboo splinters filled in with mud. The floor was uneven and cool, and the whole place smelt of Mother Earth. It was a pleasing smell, and seemed to take us back to some primeval simplicity, intimately bound up with earth and mud and dust. Along the wall was a sort of running ledge covered with a crazy variety of objects: cardboard houses, paper flowers, clumsy drawings and head work. 'These are the works of children who have studied here, and some of them have a special significance: presented to me by the outgoing children or the very special effort of a child. They are the trophies of this school. I consider them a real source of joy. For instance, the very first work of a child has some peculiar value. I don't know if others understand that there is anything in it at all . . . you will understand it better if I say look at that green paper boat. Can you guess who has made it? Your daughter on the very first day she came here, she finished it within an hour.'

I felt thrilled. Beside a parrot cut out of a cardboard picture and an inkpot made of paper, this green boat stood. I went over and picked it up. My little Leela in relation to an outside world, making her own mark on it: I was filled with pride and satisfaction. 'It is a whaler with a knife-edge at the keel!' I cried in joy. He jumped out of his seat: 'That's what I say. See how lovely it is!' The sight of it filled him with a mystic ecstasy. 'She is a grand child. So are the other children. The first work of almost every child is here and the other works go into the general hall.' The walls were hung with different pictures, tigers and lions and trees drawn with childish hands. He swept his hands about and declared: 'Every one of these is children's work. They are the real gods on earth.' He stopped before each picture and enjoyed the thrill of it anew. He had done away with tables and chairs. In a corner he had seats for visitors. 'This will do for a school. We are a poor country, and we can do without luxuries. Why do we want anything more than a shed and a few mats and open air? This is not a cold country for all the heavy furniture and elaborate buildings. This has cost me just fifty rupees, and I had three such built. But we have not much use for them, most of our time being spent outside, under the tree.'

'I'm sorry,' he said. 'Sit down, sit down. I wanted to show you the stories I've made ...' He pulled out a box and brought out a big bundle of brown paper: huge pages covered with letters as well as figures cut out and pasted. 'This is a new method which I find fascinating,' he said. 'I invent a story, write it down in words, and illustrate it with pictures cut out of illustrated books and papers and pasted, at the appropriate places; for instance this,' he threw down ten volumes, 'is a pretty long story of a bison and a tiger in the forest ... just glance through it.' Every page had a figure or two; the illustrations ran along with the story.

'They are almost real you know,' he said as I gazed on the pictures. 'Just watch, I'll show you how it works.' He stood in the doorway and announced: 'Story! Story!' The children who had been playing about, stopped, looked at him and came running in, uttering shrieks of joy.

They sat around their master. When they subsided into silence he opened the large album and said looking at it: 'This is the story of a tiger and his friend the jungle buffalo, called Bison. It happened in Mempi Forest. Who can tell me where Mempi Forest is?' There followed a discussion among the children and one girl said pointing at the doorway: 'There, near those mountains, am I right?'

'Right, right,' he said. 'There are a lot of jungles there. See here.' All the children leaned over each other's shoulders and fixed their eyes on the top of the album where a perfect jungle had been made with the help of dry tinted grass pasted together. 'These are all bamboo jungles, full of tigers, but we are only concerned with one tiger. His name is Raja. See this. There he is, a young cub.'

'He is very young,' said the children, looking at him. The album was passed round for the benefit of those sitting far off. 'What a fearful fellow!' commented a few. My daughter, sitting between two friends older than herself, refused to touch the album because of the tiger, but was quite prepared to see it if held by her neighbour. 'This little tiger was quite lonely, you know, because her mother had been taken away by hunters— bad fellows.' Thus the story of the tiger went on. The tiger came across a friend in the shape of a young bison, who protected him from a bear and other enemies. They both lived in a cave at the tail end of Mempi Hills—great friends. The bison grew up into a thick rock-like animal, and the tiger also grew up and went out in search of prey at nights. One night a party of hunters shot at the bison and carried him off to the town. And the tiger missed his friend and his cry rang through the Mempi Forest the whole night. The tiger soon adjusted himself to a lonely existence.

The children listened in dead silence and were greatly moved when this portion was read out. They all came over to have a look at the tiger in his loneliness, and our friend, rightly guessing that they would ask for it, had procured a picture. The tiger was standing forlorn before his cave. The children uttered many cries of regret and unhappiness. 'Master, how can he live without his friend any more? I hope he is not killed by the bear!'

'No. No, that bear was disposed of by the friend before he was caught.'

'Poor bear! Let me have a look at him,' said a girl. The pages were turned back and there he was, dark and shaggy. 'He could have fought with the bison. He looks so strong,' said the girl. She was, somehow, unaccountably, on the side of the bear. 'You should not like the bear,' said another girl. 'The teacher will be angry if you like the bear ...'

'No, no, I won't be. You may like what you like,' said the teacher. This was an inducement for another child to join the ranks of bear-lovers. She said: 'I always like a bear. It has such a lot of hair. Who will comb her hair, teacher?' 'Of course, her mother,' said another child.

'Has she a mother? Poor thing, yet she was allowed to be killed by the bison. I don't like bisons. They should have more hair!'

'If you are so fond of bears, why do you listen to this story?'

'Because it's the story of a bear, of course,' replied the child.

'It isn't.'

'It is. You see the picture.'

'Master, she is looking too long at the bear. I want to see the tiger.' The teacher interfered at this stage and restored order. He whispered to me: 'The most enchanting thing among children is their quarrels. How they carry it on for its own sake, without the slightest bitterness or any memory of it later. This is how we were once, God help us: this too is what we have turned out to be!' He resumed the story. My daughter, who felt she had left me alone too long, came over and sat with her elbows resting on my lap. She whispered: 'Father, I want a tiger.'

'A real one?'

'Yes. Isn't it like a cat?' I nudged the teacher, and told him of her demand. He became very serious and said: 'You must not think of a tiger as a pet, darling. It

140

is a very big and bad animal. I will show you a tiger when a circus comes to the town next. Meanwhile you may have a picture of a tiger. I will give you one.'

'All right, master, I will take it.'

'And you can have a real cat. I will give you a small kitten I have at home.'

She screamed with joy. 'Is it in your house?'

'Yes, yes. I will give it to you and also the picture of a tiger.'

'Father, let us go with him ...'

'Surely, surely,' the teacher looked delighted. 'Come with me ...' He went on for a few minutes more and ceased. The story would run on for a full week. He stopped because the clock had struck twelve. The children wouldn't get up. The tiger had just been caught by a circus man for training. The children wanted to know more and more. 'Master, you mustn't stop. What happens to the tiger? Is he happy?' He would answer none of their questions. He ruthlessly shut his books and got up.

'We are hungry, teacher. We will go home.'

'That's why I stopped the story. Go home and come and listen to it tomorrow,' he said.

'Do they kill the tiger?' asked one child.

'No, no, he is quite safe. He will be quite all right, trust me,' said the teacher. The children, greatly pleased, ran out of the school. My daughter asked: 'Is it the same circus you promised to take me to?'

'Ah, something like it. Here too you will see a tiger,' he replied and we got up. He locked the shed and the gate and walked down with us. When we reached our house, my daughter insisted upon going with him though she was hungry. He cajoled and coaxed her to go in. But she was adamant. At which he offered to come in and wait for the girl to finish her food and then take her with him. I seated him in my study.

'This is the book I read,' the girl said, placing the big catalogue in his hand. He turned over its leaves and was lost in its pictures. I took her in to dine. I told the old lady: 'There is another person for lunch today. Can you manage?'

'Oh, yes,' she said, although I knew she'd give her share of food or cook again. I invited the headmaster to sit down with me. He looked happy and at the same time uncomfortable: 'My wife at home, she will be waiting . . .'

'Won't she guess you won't be in?' I asked. 'Come on.' He yielded.

It was a most delightful party. I found him more and more fascinating. He took off his coat, folded up his sleeves, and asked: 'Where is the bathroom? I should like to have a wash.' He came out of the bathroom and said (his face wet with water and hands dripping): 'Don't offer me a towel please . . .'

'Then how do you dry it?'

'I just leave it alone, and it will evaporate. I never use a towel.'

'Why, fear of infection?'

'I don't know. I have never liked a towel, not even my own. Even after a bath I just keep standing till the water evaporates, and then put on my dress with the result that every day my wife creates a most fearful row outside the bathroom, because you know it takes a little time for a wholesale drying like that.'

My daughter was delighted that her teacher was eating with us. She was sitting down in her place with her silver plate in front of her, and was halfway through her rice. But when she saw her teacher she exclaimed with joy: 'I will also eat with teacher,' and tried to get up. She was, however, pressed back into her seat. She was very unhappy. 'Eat slowly, but don't get up. Eat slowly till your teacher joins us,' I said. The teacher would want some more time for himself. 'Please grant me fifteen minutes. I usually pray and meditate for fifteen minutes before I eat, the only time that I can spare. Just fifteen minutes ... Another thing that seems to upset my wife.' His wife seemed to be weighing on his mind. He muttered: 'I could have managed well as a bachelor, but they wouldn't let me alone.' There was something very appealing in the way he spoke. He spoke of himself as if it were someone else. His own life seemed to give him as much amusement as he found the company of children inspiring. I found a place for him to sit and meditate, left him alone and came away. He preferred the back courtyard facing the east. He squatted on the floor and closed his eyes and was lost in it. He was completely wrapped in his own vision for quite a long while, and then came and joined me. He did not seem to have the slightest feeling of being in a stranger's house. He conducted himself as if he were in his own house. As he came into the dining room and took his seat on the plank next to mine he asked: 'What have you done for lunch? I hope I have not put you to great difficulty or extra trouble?'

'Oh, no. Some simple fare. I hope you won't find it too bad . . .'

My daughter remarked: 'Our master doesn't look like himself without his coat.' He usually wore a loose, colourless coat, buttoned up to his neck. Now without it he certainly looked different. He looked rather young and slight. He seemed to put away ten years when he took off his coat. Indistinct features, greying at the temples, pouches under the red eyes. With all this there was a touch of freshness about him. My daughter asked: 'Tell me a story, teacher.'

'No, no, we must never tell stories while eating. Only at school. What should we do at school, if we had spent all the stories at home while eating?'

After food he reclined on the mat in the hall. My daughter placed before him a plate of betel leaves and areca nut. He chewed them with contentment. His lips became as red as his eyes. He looked very happy. The child sat nestling close to him and exhibited to him all her toys: the scores of coloured utensils, and brass miniature vessels, the rubber balls and her big doll. She carried the doll on her arm and said: 'This girl wants to come with me every day to school. She cries and shouts every day. What shall I do, master?'

He looked at the doll and said: 'Not a bad girl.' He pretended to pinch its cheeks and said: 'See how soft she is . . .' My daughter was greatly pleased. She looked at the doll affectionately and said: 'She is a most lovely girl, master. But she does want to go with me to school, what shall I do?'

'Do you want to bring her or not?' She shook her head sadly. 'No, master. She is a bad baby and will give a lot of trouble at the school. She will not allow me to study there. She will quarrel with everyone.' Certain inescapable anti-social characteristics of this doll seemed to sadden Leela, but she had steeled herself to a sort of resignation. So her teacher said: 'Well, why don't you lock her up in a box when you come to school?' Leela shook her head: 'That I can't do because she will die. I will lock her up in a room.'

The teacher asked: 'Do you mind if I lie down and rest a while?' He lay down and shut his eyes. My daughter insisted upon lying down beside him. Soon she was fast asleep. So was he. I went away to my room, picked up a book, lay on my camp easy chair, and dozed.

We were all ready to start out at four in the afternoon, my daughter persistently asking for the cat.

A TIGER IN THE SCHOOL

[The novel A Tiger for Malgudi *is the first-person account of Raja, a tiger who has escaped from captivity and strayed into the town of Malgudi. The following excerpt is a hilarious account of the chaos that ensues when the tiger takes refuge in a school, and a professional shikari is hired to go after it.]*

IT WAS STILL a busy hour in the city when I entered Market Road. People ran for their lives at the sight of me. As I progressed through, shutters were pulled down, and people hid themselves under culverts, on trees, behind pillars. The population was melting out of sight. At the circus I had had no chance to study human behaviour. Outside the circus ring they sat in their seats placidly while I cowered before Captain's whip. I got a totally wrong notion of human beings at that angle. I had thought that they were sturdy and fearless. But now I found them fleeing before me like a herd of deer, although I had no intention of attacking them. When I paused in front of a tailor's shop, he abandoned his machine and shut himself in a cupboard, wailing, 'Alas, I am undone, won't someone shoot that tiger?' A prisoner between two constables, who had been caught for murder and was just emerging from the Court House, got his chance to escape when the constables fled, abandoning him with his handcuffs. I tore a horse from its jutka and enjoyed the sight of the passengers spilling out of it and running for their lives. A couple of street dogs invited destruction when they barked madly, instead of minding their business.

Later, I learnt from my master of the chaos that befell the city when it became known that Captain had been destroyed and that I was somewhere in the city. Sheer hopelessness seems to have seized the townspeople. They withdrew to their homes and even there remained nervous. All doors and windows everywhere were shut, bolted, and sealed. Some even thought that I was some extraordinary creature who might pass through the walls and lie in wait on the roof or in the loft or basement. Poor people living in huts had real cause to worry: I could have taken any of their homes apart. But why should I? One could understand their fears, but why should those living in brick and cement feel nervous? It was due to their general lack of a sense of security and an irrational dread of losing their assets. Why should an ordinary simple tiger have any interest in them either to destroy or to safeguard?

I rested for a moment at the door of Anand Bhavan, on Market Road, where coffee drinkers and tiffin eaters at their tables sat transfixed, uttering low moans on seeing me. I wanted to assure them, 'Don't fear, I am not out to trouble you. Eat your tiffin in peace, don't mind me ... You, nearest to me, hugging the cash box, you are craven with fear, afraid even to breathe. Go on, count the cash, if that's your pleasure. I just want to watch, that's all ... If my tail trails down to the street, if I am blocking your threshold, it is because, I'm told, I'm eleven feet tip to tail. I can't help it. I'm not out to kill ... I'm too full—found a green pasture teeming with food on the way. Won't need any for several days to come, won't stir, not until I feel hungry again. Tigers attack only when they feel hungry, unlike human beings who slaughter one another without purpose or hunger ...'

To the great delight of children, schools were being hurriedly closed. Children of all ages and sizes were running helter-skelter, screaming joyously, 'No school, no school. Tiger, tiger!' They were shouting and laughing and even enjoyed being scared. They seemed to welcome me. I felt like joining them, and bounded away from the restaurant door and trotted along with them, at which they gleefully cried, 'The tiger is coming to eat us; let us get back to the school!'

I followed them through their school gate while they ran up and shut themselves in the school hall securely. I ascended the steps of the school, saw an open door at the far end of a veranda, and walked in. It happened to be the headmaster's room, I believe, as I noticed a very dignified man jumping on his table and heaving himself up into an attic. I walked in and flung myself on the cool floor, having a partiality for cool stone floor, with my head under the large desk—which gave me the feeling of being back in the Mempi cave . . . As I drowsed, I was aware of cautious steps and hushed voices all around. I was in no mood to bother about anything. All I wanted was a little moment of sleep; the daylight was dazzling. In half sleep I heard the doors of the room being shut and bolted and locked. I didn't care. I slept.

While I slept a great deal of consultation was going on. I learnt about it later through my master, who was in the crowd—the crowd which had gathered after making sure that I had been properly locked up—and was watching. The headmaster seems to have remarked some days later, 'Never dreamt in my wildest mood that I'd have to yield my place to a tiger . . .' A wag had retorted, 'Might be one way of maintaining better discipline among the boys.'

'Now that this brute is safely locked up, we must decide,' began a teacher.

At this moment my master pushed his way through the crowds and admonished, 'Never use the words "beast" or "brute". They're ugly words coined by man in his arrogance. The human being thinks all other creatures are "beasts". Awful word!'

'Is this the occasion to discuss problems of vocabulary?' asked someone.

'Why not?' retorted my master. At which they looked outraged.

Someone said, 'What a reckless man you are! Who are you?'

'You are asking a profound question. I've no idea who I am! All my life I have been trying to find the answer. Are you sure you know who you are?'

'Crazy beggar—with a tiger in there ready to devour us, but for the strong door ... There is no time for useless talk. Let us get on with the business ...'

'What business? What is it going to be?' asked my master.

Everyone was upset at this question. 'We must think of those children shut in the hall,' said a teacher.

'Open the door and let them out,' said my master, unasked.

'Not your business to advise us; who are you?'

'Second time you are asking the same question. I say again, I don't know,' said my master.

'Get out of the school premises,' said a man who acted for the headmaster in his absence. 'You have no business here. We can't have all kinds of intruders . . .'

'Did the tiger come on your invitation?' asked my master.

'We have to think seriously what to do now. Please leave us alone. Go away, I say,' commanded the acting headmaster.

At which my master said, 'A headmaster must be obeyed in his school, even if he is only acting,' and slipped back to the farthest end of the veranda.

'Go away,' they all shouted.

'I'll stay, but promise not to disturb your consultations . . .' And then my master withdrew to a far corner to watch them, to observe how they were going to tackle the tiger. They constantly turned their heads and threw furtive looks at him, feeling uneasy to talk in his presence, but at the same time finding it difficult to order him out. They lowered their voices. The acting headmaster said, 'Now we have to decide on the next step to take . . .'

'Yes, yes,' chorused his assistant masters.

'We must get someone to shoot it. Who has a gun in our town?' Everyone fell into deep thinking. The mathematics teacher, the most practical-minded in the institution, said, 'I'm sure the police will have it. Send someone to fetch the superintendent.'

I must have turned in my sleep and knocked over some piece of furniture and that seemed to have scared them further. All of them cried, 'Let us go, it is perhaps trying to break open the door!' and started to retreat desperately.

At this point my master shouted from his corner, 'He can't open the door. He has no hands. Only some furniture . . .'

Whereupon they glared at him and said, 'If you are going to be here, take care not to interrupt our talks.'

My master, being calm and wise, merely said, 'Very well, I won't interrupt.'

The mathematics teacher now said, 'Shall I call the police to handle the tiger?'

Another teacher had a misgiving at this point: 'I doubt if this is a police matter. No law has been broken . . .'

'Is it lawful to let loose a tiger in a public thoroughfare?'

'Who let it loose? No one. It came by itself.'

'The circus man is responsible.'

'But he is dead . . . They must arrest the film producer for endangering public safety.'

'Where are they? They have all vanished—fled before the tiger . . . took their shattered cameras too . . . We can't go after them now. I wouldn't be surprised if the tiger has swallowed them up . . .'

'I wouldn't think so,' said my master again. 'He is not a maneater . . .'

'Isn't he? Have you tested him?' asked the acting headmaster, rather viciously, annoyed at the fact that the man was still there.

My master said, 'I don't notice any progress in your talk. Why don't you let all the children go home without making any noise . . . and all of you may also go home . . .'

'And leave the tiger in charge of the school?' asked the acting headmaster with an untimely irony. And added, 'You must go. We don't want you on the premises, whatever we may decide . . .' he said, glaring at my master.

At which my master shouted back, 'If my presence is the real problem rather than the tiger, I'll go, but you will see me again, I have no doubt,' rather mysteriously and went off. All eyes followed him till he disappeared beyond the school gate. My master was only out of their vision, but was at hand, sitting on a culvert keenly watching the goings-on at the school veranda, not missing a single word of their confused babble. He heard, 'Get a gun immediately.'

'Does anyone know how to shoot?'

'The superintendent of police has a gun . . .'

'But he can't use it unless a magistrate orders . . .'

'Where does he live? He used to be in the New

Extension ... that yellow house in the Third Cross corner.'

'Now he has moved to the government quarters ...'

'Better we get Alphonse. He is a good shikari, licensed double-barrelled gun. The walls of his house are covered with bison heads and stuff like that. He's a good shot.'

'But he is a declared poacher; they have confiscated his gun.'

'Can't be, I saw him yesterday at Market Gate ...'

'Did you see him with a gun?'

'Why should he take his gun to the market? I spoke to him and he said he was going to camp in the forest the next four days—'

'It is rumoured that they have taken away his hunting licence ...'

'But he said he was shooting with a camera.'

'His camera may shoot bullets, too. Don't you believe such fellows—they are really poachers.'

Now I let out a growl, a mild one, and that brought their minds back to the business on hand.

'Better get the DFO.'

'What is DFO?'

'You mean you don't know DFO means District Forest Officer?' At which the man thus corrected was annoyed, and insults and angry words were exchanged until the acting headmaster intervened and reminded them that they were engaging themselves in an untimely wasteful talk. And then he turned to the school servant to ask, 'Do you know where the DFO lives?'

'No, sir,' he said promptly.

A student came forward—a young fellow who had managed to stay back when all others had rushed into the school hall. 'Ravi is my friend, I know where he lives.'

'Who is Ravi?' His answer was drowned in a lot of cross-talk.

'Don't forget the HM can't come down. How long can he be crouching in that loft?'

'How are you sure that he climbed into the loft?'

'They had a glimpse while shutting the door ... Don't waste time in this sort of cross-examination.'

They seemed to be incapable of reaching any practical solution. My master, who had been sitting on the culvert, came back to say, 'If you keep chatting like this, I'll dash up and let the tiger out ...'

'Oh, would you? You will be the first fellow to be devoured,' said an idiot. And all the members said, 'We said you should keep out of here, why have you come back?'

'Just to see if you fellows will do or say anything useful. Pity the children whose education and training are in your hands ...'

At which the acting headmaster drew himself up to

say, 'Get out of this place, this is our school. In the absence of the headmaster, I take his place automatically. I have told you that already.'

'Yes, yes, I remember; you have also said that when a headmaster, even if he is only acting, gives an order, it must be obeyed instantly,' and he went back to his seat on the culvert at the gate, beyond their range of vision but not out of earshot.

Presently he saw a man arrive on a noisy motor cycle, drowning all other sounds, carrying a gun. He slowed down near my master to ask excitedly, 'I heard of a tiger being somewhere here—is it true?'

My master indicated the school, but added, 'You can't shoot him, if that's your idea . . .' Ignoring him, the man turned into the gate with a haughty toss of his head.

Now my master followed a fresh motley crowd drifting in, driven by a mixture of curiosity and fear. Now that they knew the tiger was locked up, throngs of men and women were in the streets purposelessly wandering about and vaguely looking for the tiger. All normal activity in the city was suspended. In the crowd one could find lawyers in their black gowns, shopmen who had pulled down the shutters, hawkers with trays on their heads, policemen in uniform, and so forth. The school had never seen such a crowd before in its compound and veranda. An army of anxious parents arrived, desperately searching for their children. They dashed hither and thither and towards the headmaster's room in a body, demanding, 'Where are our children? We want our children safely back. What sort of a school is this that they can't protect our children when a tiger is about?'

A teacher was provoked by this remark. 'Why do you presume such things? Haven't we a responsibility?'

'Where are our children? My child is only seven years old. It's a mistake to have sent him to this wretched tiger-infested school.'

'You perhaps are always ready to attack the school . . .'

A burly parent came up shaking his fist. 'Don't go on philosophizing. We don't want your philosophy. Where are the children? You should have closed the school when the tiger was known to have escaped into the town. If anything happens to the child, I'll smash you all and set fire to the school.'

The teacher looked scared between a bully and the tiger. He said in a trembling voice, 'We let them off early, but they came back.'

Meanwhile a group, having heard the shouts of the children locked up in the hall, went up and forced open the door, and the children poured out of the room like flood water released from a sluice, screaming and roaring with joy. Confusion was at its maximum.

The man with the gun strode in with the gun in position, shouting at the top of his voice: 'Keep away, everybody. I won't be responsible if anyone is hurt. I'll count. Before I count ten, everyone must clear out of the way. Otherwise I will shoot and won't be responsible for any mishap to any individual,' and he held up and flourished his double-barrelled gun, asking, 'Is he in there? I can shoot through the door . . .'

'Oh, no, don't. The headmaster is also in there.'

'He went up into the loft and is crouching there . . .'

'I'll aim and hit right on it, only the tiger. You may keep a flower on its back or even the headmaster himself, but my bullet will leave everything else untouched and bring down the beast alone.'

At this moment my master came forward to say, 'Never use that word again . . .'

'Which word?' asked Alphonse the gunman.

' "Beast" is an ugly, uncharitable expression.'

'Mind your business.'

'This is my business,' answered my master, and people, fearing that he might be shot, pulled him away. The gunman continued his plans.

'But how are you to know where he is in that room?'

'If the door is pushed open slightly, I can immediately—'

'If the tiger dashes out?'

'Oh, a moving target is no problem. I have brought down creatures running at one hundred miles an hour . . .'

'No, no, opening the door is out of the question, impossible.'

'Get me a ladder, then. I'll go up and shoot from the roof . . . enough if a couple of tiles are removed . . .' Someone was hustled to fetch a ladder from a neighbouring house. They all waited in silence. Somehow the sight of the gunman seemed to have subdued the crowd. They spoke in hushed voices. 'Where is the ladder?' demanded Alphonse. 'Who is gone to fetch one?' he asked with an air of command. People looked at each other, and no one came up with an answer. At which Alphonse stamped his foot like a spoilt child, and demanded angrily, 'Who is in charge here?' The acting headmaster was unwilling to come forward now, with the tiger on one side and the gun-wielder on the other. He had tried to make himself obscure and slip away unnoticed. But others seized him by his arm and propelled him forward, crying, 'Here is the first assistant, he is in charge when the headmaster is away.'

The acting headmaster said, 'The HM is still there in his room. He is not away actually.'

'Oh, oh,' someone jeered.

'But is he in a position to issue orders?'

'Perhaps not—may not be audible if he talks from

inside the tiger,' a wag suggested. And there was giggling all round.

At this my master came forward to ask, 'Is this the time for levity?'

Alphonse turned on him fiercely. 'Who are you?'

My master said, 'Oh, once again the same question! I wish I could answer with so many asking the same question.'

'I am not prepared to waste time talking to you ... Now be off. Don't interrupt, I don't care who you are or what you are ... you loincloth-covered, bearded loon ...' He then turned his attention to the acting headmaster and asked sternly, 'Are you in charge of this school?'

'Yes, only when the headmaster is on leave. Not when he is in there ...' He pointed at the headmaster's room.

Alphonse glared at him and said, 'I know you are trying to be slippery. Heaven help you if you are going to be tricky. I like people to be straightforward and truthful ... You are the man in charge. If you think you are going to have your chance to take his place by letting him be eaten up, you are mistaken. I am determined to get him out intact—if I have to shoot down everything in my way, I'll do it. Now get me a ladder. It's urgent.' The acting headmaster was speechless; the crowd watched in a state of hushed awe. Some persons were trying to leave, unable to judge how the situation might develop and anticipating bloodshed. Alphonse held the acting headmaster with his look and demanded, 'Get me a ladder at once.'

'We have no ladder in this school,' he said timidly.

'Do you mean to say,' Alphonse asked contemptuously, 'that you run a school like this without a ladder?'

'What is a ladder for in a teaching institution?' questioned the acting headmaster in a foolhardy manner.

'Don't be impudent,' said Alphonse, glaring at him, at which the acting headmaster took fright and tried to mollify him by saying, 'Headmaster requisitioned for one last year, but the DPI's office are holding up the sanction. Unless they sanction the budget, we can't even buy a pin . . .'

'The procedure is silly,' commented Alphonse.

A few others murmured, 'True, sir, we all agree with you. We can't buy even a cane except through the DPI's sanction.'

'What do you want a cane for?' demanded Alphonse, going off at a tangent. 'Do you mean to say you are using it on the boys? Whenever I find teachers doing that, I give them a taste of it first . . .'

'Oh, no, I just mentioned cane because it came to my mind. We never do such things . . . We get cattle straying into our garden and we use the stick to drive them away.'

'Hmm . . . you had better be careful. If you teachers wish to save your skins, remember I'll as readily bag wild pedagogues as I do wild animals of the forest.'

'Educational norms are different today.'

'What do you mean by it?' Alphonse asked severely, turning to the speaker.

'We have to handle them psychologically . . .'

'Good for you, keep it in mind.'

At this point two boys came through carrying a bamboo ladder between them and placed it before the crowd. Alphonse was delighted. He patted the boys' heads by turn, one by one, methodically. 'Where have you got this from?' he asked, very pleased.

'We ran to a house in Kabir Lane, I had noticed that they had kept a ladder in their backyard, to pluck drumsticks from the tree, and now they had locked themselves in and also shut all the windows because of the tiger, and so I brought it away quietly and they did not see us. I was dragging it along, but Ramu saw me on the way and helped me and both of us carried it down—because we heard you asking for a ladder, I ran out at once, remembering the ladder in the next house . . .'

'You are a very intelligent, observant fellow. What is your name?'

'Shekar,' he answered proudly and loudly.

'Shekar,' cried Alphonse enthusiastically. 'Come

163

and see me with your friend. I'll have a present for you. I've a wonderful air-gun, with which you can practise. You won't need a licence for it although you can hit and disable a buck at forty feet . . . Our country needs more boys of your type. You are our only hope.'

'He is the brightest fellow in our school,' the acting headmaster ventured to suggest with some pride, to please the gunman.

'I'm glad you recognize it, if you really mean it. Shekar, you and your friend take the ladder over there and put it up for me to go up to the roof . . .'

One couldn't have secured more spirited helpers. Shekar and Ramu felt so flattered that they were prepared to obey any command from Uncle Alphonse. 'He has promised me a gun. I'll shoot all the crows and dogs in our street.'

'I'll shoot the donkeys,' said Ramu.

'How can you?' Shekar asked. 'He has only one gun and that is promised to me.'

'It's for both of us,' Ramu said. 'Let us share it.'

'How can two shoot with a single gun?' sneered Shekar, but before this could develop into a full-scale argument, Alphonse cried, 'Come on, boys, march on with the ladder.'

The two boys took the ladder out to the spot indicated, and Alphonse placed it below the eaves of the headmaster's office. He then turned to a small crowd, which followed him. He braced himself for the task, put one foot on the first rung, and turned to face his audience: 'You must all be calm and mind your business if you have any. Don't get panicky if you hear gunshots presently. I can shoot straight and, finally I'll get him, of course, but there can be no guarantee how the tiger will behave when he is hit. Before I send the second shot and dispatch him, he may go mad and devilish and storm his way out of the room, he may spring skyward, or dash through the door or break the walls in his fury. One can't foresee what'll happen then, especially when I have not seen the brute—'

'He is no brute,' shouted my master from back of the crowd. 'No more than any of us here.'

'Ah, ah! You are still here. You were ordered to remain out of range, weren't you? Anyway if you are still here you will see who is a brute when he comes out. However, if you have no business here, get out of this place smartly . . . I want two men up here to come up with me and loosen the tiles. If I see clearly inside, I can finish the job in a moment.'

'What about the headmaster, who must be somewhere between your gun and the animal?'

'That's a problem,' said Alphonse generously, 'but if you have confidence in me, he'll escape the shot.'

'But the tiger may spring up, you said, and God knows where he will be caught,' said someone.

Alphonse said, 'Don't imagine troubles. Have you confidence in me or not?' He paused and waited for an answer. It was Shekar who shouted at the top of his voice, 'Don't let them stop you, Uncle, go on and shoot the animal. I'd love to see how you shoot.'

'Follow me then and help to remove the tiles. I'll tell you how to do it . . . The grown-ups here are all cowards and ought to wear sarees; they are afraid to see a tiger even from a rooftop.'

'I'm not afraid,' said Shekar, and his friend added a confirmation. Alphonse climbed the ladder, followed by the two boys, who were cautioned and admonished by their teachers for their foolhardiness.

'If I had four arms like some of your gods,' said Alphonse from the roof, 'I would not have needed the help of these young people. Two of my hands would have pulled the tiles out, while the other two might have been holding the gun and triggering off the shot. Four arms are a most sensible arrangement.' And then he proceeded to remove a few tiles and asked the boys to follow his example. They tore up the tiles with zest and threw them down recklessly, enjoying the sight of their elders dodging below.

Soon an opening was made, and a shaft of sunlight entered the room. The headmaster was on the point of collapse, crouching there in the narrow attic, amidst bundles of old papers and files. He looked up and saw the faces of the two boys on the roof and could not make out what they were doing up there. He could not believe his eyes. He tried to stand up, but hit his head on the rafters. Shekar cried, 'It's me, sir. My friend is also here, Ramu of 4B. Uncle is here to shoot the tiger . . .' The headmaster had enough wits about him to understand the situation. 'Sir, aren't you hungry? If you come out, I'll run up to Pankaja Cafe and bring you tiffin, if someone gives me money,' said the boy.

The headmaster took his finger to his lips to warn the boy not to make a noise and wake up the tiger. He spoke in a hoarse whisper. At the mention of the tiger, Shekar was pushed aside and in his place the headmaster found another head. 'I'm Alphonse,' said the man. 'Headmaster, keep cool; we will get you out soon. Ah! I see him there . . . must be eleven-point-five feet . . . a full-grown brute. Wish his head were not under the table. I could dispatch him with one shot then and there. You need have no doubt . . . I could shoot now, but if he is hit in the hind part, he may go mad and spring up. I've seen such beasts go up even fifteen feet in the air under similar circumstances. But first let me get you out of here . . . Keep cool . . . don't fall off the attic.' He looked around. 'Boy, you must run and get a hacksaw or an ordinary carpenter's saw. Run and get it as smartly as you brought the ladder. If you see a carpenter, snatch it from his bag.'

'Yes, you will need more than a carpenter's saw,' said a voice, and turning round Alphonse exclaimed, 'You, here still!'

'Yes, yes,' said my master. 'I could come up a ladder as well as anyone.'

'Weren't you told to keep out?' asked Alphonse angrily.

'Yes, yes,' agreed my master amiably, and added, 'Who are you to pass such orders?'

'You are a pertinacious pest,' remarked Alphonse in disgust. 'Now the urgent thing is that you get the saw. You stick like the burr, but at least make yourself useful . . . go and get a saw immediately.'

'What for?'

Alphonse suppressed his irritation, and said, 'I want to saw off a couple of those crossbars, enough to admit the headmaster's head, and then we could pull him out and tackle the tiger.'

'And you expect the tiger to watch the fun while you are at your carpentry?' my master said with a smile.

Alphonse said, 'If you do not behave, I'll push you in through this gap. Shekar, get a saw without delay—instead of listening to this mad fellow. He is persistent . . . No way of keeping him off.'

'How can you keep me off? Who are you?' asked my master, and added, 'I can ask the same question you asked, who are you? I know enough law to realize that I have as good a right to be on a roof as anyone else!'

'I'm only here to help the headmaster ...'

'You won't be able to work through the rafters so easily. They are old teak beams. You will have to saw for days before you can make a dent ...'

'In that case, I'll shoot. I've enough sight now. Let the headmaster stay where he is, and take his chance and pray for his life and pray that the tiger does not spring up vertically ...' He turned to the headmaster, who was peering out like a prisoner behind the bars: 'Only be careful that you don't fall off the edge when you hear my gun go off, stick close to the wall so that even if the tiger springs up, you will stay clear of his reach. With the second, I'll get him, even if he is in mid-air ...'

'Oh, here they are,' exclaimed my master, pointing at the school gate. A jeep had arrived at the gate and a number of persons jumped out of it and hurried across the school compound. They pushed their way through the crowd.

'Come down, please, and keep your finger off the trigger. We are the Save Tiger Committee. You must hear us first. We are a statutory body with police powers ...'

Alphonse came down the ladder, saying, 'The

headmaster is about to be saved. Please give me five minutes, I'll get him out and then we can discuss.'

The wild-life committee paused to consider it for a moment, and asked, 'Explain how you propose to save the headmaster.'

Alphonse explained that he proposed to cut through the rafters and bail out the headmaster.

My master, who had followed him down, said, 'Rafters are of ancient timber, it'll take at least three days to make a notch.'

Alphonse glared at him and exclaimed, 'You again! Why do you dog my steps like this? I'd knock you down with the butt, but for your age. The animal is there already stirring and growling. How long do you think the headmaster will stand the tension? He may faint and roll off the attic straight into the mouth of the tiger. You won't let me call him a beast. I don't know why I'm being plagued by you ... you follow me like a shadow ...'

My master ignored Alphonse and turned to the visitors: 'I'm grateful that you have responded to my call. If you hadn't come, he'd have murdered the tiger. His plan was to make enough noise with a saw or anything to stir up the animal, and shoot, leaving it to chance for the headmaster to survive ...'

Alphonse ground his teeth and remained silent. Meanwhile Shekar plucked at his sleeve. 'Uncle, give me money, I'll buy idli and vadai at the Pankaja Cafe for the headmaster . . .' Alphonse fished out of his pocket a rupee and gave it to the boy, who at once ran off. Alphonse said, looking after him, 'This fellow is the hope of our country. He is fit to ride on the back of a tiger . . .'

The leader of the wild-life group said, 'Mr Alphonse, as you may be aware, I'm the chairman of the local chapter of Tiger Project, affiliated to the Central Committee under the Ministry of Agriculture at Delhi . . .'

'What has agriculture to do with tigers?' asked Alphonse.

'We will go into the question later, but at the moment we wish to emphasize the fact that Save Tiger Project, as its name indicates, is to prevent the decimation of the tiger population which was at one time in the neighbourhood of 15,000 today it's less than 1,500.' He went into statistics until Alphonse said, 'Is this the time for a lecture, while the headmaster is half dead inside? You think that only tigers are important and not a headmaster . . .'

'And so,' continued the chairman, 'there is a general ordinance issued by the government which prohibits the shooting of any tiger, in any part of India, and we are given powers to enforce the rules and initiate prosecution if and when necessary; with penalty up to

Rs 2,000 and one year's rigorous imprisonment and confiscation of the offender's weapon and licence . . .'

'I know all this and more,' said Alphonse. 'You are opening your eyes on this subject probably only now. But I have been in the tiger business for half a century. There's a provision in the same ordinance, an exemption where a man-eater is concerned . . .'

'Yes, yes, we know all that; where a tiger has been established to be a man-eater, we can permit the shooting, provided you apply for it with proof and evidence . . .'

'What proof? Remains of a poor villager snatched away from the tiger's jaw? I'll also have to file a photograph and write an application in triplicate, I suppose?' Alphonse asked, with grim humour. 'You and your government regulations. You have no practical sense . . . You'll see half the population destroyed in your zeal to protect the tiger: perhaps that's a ruse to keep down the population of our country! Ha! Ha! Ha! Here's a headmaster struggling to survive and you go on talking rules. You people do not distinguish between what's important and unimportant.'

Meanwhile I awoke after a very good stretch of sleep and heard voices outside. I looked up and saw the headmaster cowering in the attic. I stretched myself and roared, for no particular reason except that I felt alive. The poor human being in the loft must have trembled at that moment. I wished to assure him that I was not going to hurt him. If it had been the old jungle days, I'd have gone after him; already a change was coming over me, I think. My master's presence in the vicinity, though he had not come near me yet, must have begun to affect me. I tried to assure the headmaster by raising myself and putting up my forelegs on the wall and scratching it, and growling softly, which must have shaken the poor man so much that he seemed to lose control of his bowels and bladder. Thereupon I withdrew from the wall and curled myself under the table once again in order to reassure the poor man.

Meanwhile, outside, my master noticed Alphonse taking the chairman aside under a tree, where they spoke in whispers. When they came back, the chairman was a changed man. He took aside, in his turn, his committee members, and spoke to them. Thereupon they took papers out of a briefcase and signed and gave them to Alphonse. All this concerned me. I was declared a man-eater and Alphonse was given written permission to shoot. 'In the normal course,' explained the chairman, 'I should get the sanction from Delhi, but in an emergency, I am empowered to use my discretion.' My master suspected that Alphonse had offered a substantial bribe, as he was known to be engaged in a flourishing business exporting tiger skins.

Shekar was seen coming down the ladder with a packet of food in hand. He approached Alphonse. 'Uncle, I can't see the headmaster; I held out the idli, but he didn't take it. What shall I do now?' 'You and Ramu shall share the idli,' said Alphonse.

The boy continued, 'I peeped and couldn't see him; I called and he wouldn't answer. I heard the tiger scratching something and growling. I came away . . .' He looked sad and anxious, moved aside and gobbled up the tiffin hurriedly.

The crowd, which watched in silence all along, let out a moan in chorus: 'Aiyo! Never thought our beloved headmaster would come to this end . . .' They all looked bitterly at the acting headmaster, who they somehow held responsible for all the delay. The acting headmaster probably had confused feelings, happy at the thought that after all he was getting his chance to become the headmaster, but also unhappy at the same time. He wailed the loudest at the thought of the headmaster's fate.

The commotion was at its height when Alphonse, properly armed with the permit, gave a final look to his double-barrelled gun, held it this way and that and looked through the barrel, and shouted a command; 'Your attention, everybody! Everyone must retreat at least a hundred yards before the school gate which will give you an initial advantage if the tiger should decide to chase. No one can foresee how the situation will develop. The beast when shot may smash the door and rush out, and God help anyone in its way. I'll count ten and this area must be cleared; otherwise, I won't be responsible for any calamity. Now all clear out . . . It's an emergency. The headmaster or whatever is left of him must be saved without delay. Now clear out, everyone.' He jingled the school-key bunch which he had snatched from the acting headmaster. 'I'm risking my life . . . I'll push the door open and shoot the same second, normally that should be enough . . .' After this he let out a shout like a cattle-driver and a stampede started towards the gate, as he started counting: 'One, two, three . . .'

He turned to the chairman and his committee and said, as a special concession, 'You may stay back in that classroom to your left and watch through the window. I've reconnoitred that area; it'll be safe for you to stay there, and you will get a good view through the window, but make sure to bolt the door.' He said to Shekar, 'Boy, show them the room and stay there yourself with your friend, until I say "all clear". He may need two shots—the interval between the first one and the second will be crucial. Anything may happen. No one can forecast with a hundred per cent certainty.'

After all these preliminaries, and before delivering the actual assault, Alphonse sat down on the veranda step and took a flask out of his hip pocket, muttering, 'This has been a big strain, must restore my nerves first . . .' He took a long swig out of it, while several pairs of eyes were watching him, smacked his lips, shook his head with satisfaction, picked up his gun and examined it keenly, and conducted a little rehearsal by pressing the butt against his shoulder and aiming at an imaginary tiger. He withdrew the gun and placed it at his side, took out the hip flask again, and took another long swig. He was heard to mutter, 'Hands are shaky, need steadying up.' And then he stood up with gun in hand, and rehearsed again with the butt against his shoulder. 'Still shaky . . . Bloody dilute rum, has no strength in it; I'll deal with that fellow.' He sat down again and took another drink, and another drink, till the flask was emptied.

My master, who had stayed back unobtrusively, came forward to ask him, 'Whom were you talking to?'

'You,' said Alphonse. 'I knew you were here. I knew you'd not go. I saw you—you obstinate devil . . . So, I thought, I thought, what did I "thought"? I don't know. I have forgotten. No, no, if the beast comes out and swallows you, it'll serve you right . . . that's what I thought. Don't look at me like that . . . I'm not drunk . . . It's only watery rum . . . less than ten per cent proof . . . I'll deal with that cheat yet . . . that bastard . . .'

'Are you relaxing?' my master asked.

'Yes, sir,' he said heartily.

And then my master asked, 'What about the tiger?'

'What about what?'

'The tiger, the tiger in there . . .'

'Oh, yes, the tiger, he is OK, I hope?'

'Aren't you going to shoot?'

'No,' he said emphatically. 'My hands must be steadied. I must have another drink. But my flask is empty. The son-of-a-bitch didn't fill it. I'll deal with him, don't worry. This sort of a thing . . .'

'The headmaster, what about him?'

'I don't know. Don't ask me. Am I responsible for every son-of a-bitch?'

'Where did you learn this rare phrase?'

'In America,' he said promptly. 'I lived there for many years.'

'Would you like to rest?'

'Of course, how did you guess? I got up at four this morning and rode fifty miles. Where is my vehicle?'

My master gave him a gentle push, and he fell flat on the ground and passed out.

My master must have turned on him his powers of suggestion. Taking the key-bunch from Alphonse, he went up to the headmaster's room and had just inserted the key into the lock when the chairman, watching through the window, shouted across at the top of his voice, 'What are you trying to do? Stop!'

'I'm only trying to get the tiger out, so that the headmaster may come down confidently.'

While this was going on Shekar suddenly threw back the bolt of the classroom and rushed out, followed by his friend Ramu. Both of them came and stood over Alphonse, watching him wide-eyed. 'He is still breathing,' one said to the other.

Both of them asked my master, 'Is Uncle dying?'

My master said to them, 'No, he will wake up—but rather late—don't worry. He will be well again . . .'

'Why is he like this? A nice uncle . . .' the boys asked tearfully.

'Oh, he will be all right,' said my master. 'Don't worry about him. He has drunk something that is not good and that has put him to sleep . . .'

'Is it toddy?' asked the boys.

'Maybe,' said my master. 'What do you know about it?'

'There is a toddy shop near our house . . .' began the boys, and my master listened patiently, while the boys described the scenes of drunkenness that they witnessed in the evenings. Finally the boys asked, 'How will he shoot the tiger?'

'No one is going to shoot,' said my master. 'You will see the tiger come out and walk off with me . . .'

'He won't eat us?'

'No, he will not hurt anyone. I'm going to open the door and bring him out.'

'The headmaster?' the boys asked anxiously.

'He must have also fallen asleep. He will also come out ... don't worry. Would you like to come in with me and see the tiger?'

The boys hesitated and, looking back for a safe spot, said, 'No, we'll stand there and watch.'

The chairman, who had watched this dialogue, cried from behind the window, 'What are you trying to do? You are mad.'

'Come out and be with me. You will see for yourself what I plan to do.'

'Explain,' the other cried. 'I do not understand you.'

My master turned round, walked to the window, and asked, 'Are you afraid to come out of that room?'

'What a question!' exclaimed the chairman. 'Of course, who wouldn't be! We are in a hurry. The headmaster must have help without delay. We must act before the gunman wakes up ...' He spoke through the window.

'Here, I have the key. I'll unlock the door and bring the tiger out of the room. One of you take a ladder in and help the headmaster come down from the attic. That's all ...'

'Do you mean to say that you are going in as you are, without arms or protection?'

'Yes, that's what I'm going to do. We have no time to waste.'

179

The chairman said, 'By the powers vested in me in my capacity as the Second Honorary Magistrate in this town, I give you notice that you shall not open or enter that room. My committee members will bear witness to this order. It comes into immediate force, notwithstanding the fact that it's not yet in written form . . .' He looked around at his members, who crowded near the window bars and assented in a chorus.

My master asked when it subsided, 'Why'll you prevent me from going near the tiger?'

They were at a loss to answer: 'It's unlawful to commit suicide.'

'Maybe,' said my master, 'but which law section says that a man should not approach a tiger? Are not circus people doing it all the time?'

'Yes,' replied the chairman weakly. 'But that's different.'

'I can tame a tiger as well as any circus ringmaster. It's after all my life that I'm risking.'

'There is no such thing as my life or your life before the eyes of the law: in the eyes of the law all lives are equal. No one can allow you to murder yourself . . .'

'Life or death is in no one's hands: you can't die by willing or escape death by determination. A great power has determined the number of breaths for each individual, who can neither stop them nor prolong . . . That's why God says in the Gita, "I'm life and death, I'm the killer and the killed . . . Those enemies you see before you, O Arjuna, are already dead, whether you aim your arrows at them or not!" '

The chairman was visibly confused and bewildered. 'In that case you will have to sign an affidavit absolving us from all responsibilities for your life or death . . .'

'You ignoramus of an honorary magistrate! After all that I have said, in spite of all that urgency . . . All right, give me a paper and tell me what to write.'

The magistrate took out a sheet of paper from his briefcase and pushed it through the window bar. My master sat down and wrote to the chairman's dictation through the window absolving anyone from any responsibility. He signed the document and returned it with the comment, 'Just to respect your magistracy, although I am convinced it's uncalled-for and irrelevant, and you are exercising unnecessary authority. The more important thing for you now would be to take in your custody that gun beside Alphonse. When he wakes up, no one can guess his mood, and it's not safe to leave the gun within his reach.'

The chairman looked at the document and said, 'Stop, wait. Tell me what is it that you have written here?'

'Only what you have dictated.'

'In a language we don't know, can't accept it . . .'

'It's in Sanskrit, in which our scriptures are written, language of the gods. I write only Sanskrit although I know ten other languages including Japanese.' Without further ado, he turned round, paused for a second to satisfy himself that Alphonse was asleep, and put the key into the lock on the headmaster's room.

I had felt provoked at the sound of the key turning in the lock. No one had a right to come in and bother me. I was enjoying my freedom, and the happy feeling that the whip along with the hand that held it was banished for ever. No more of it; it was pleasant to brood over this good fortune. It was foolish of me to have let the whip go on so long. Next time anyone displayed the whip . . . I would know what to do. Just a pat with my paw, I realized, was sufficient to ward off any pugnacious design. What ignorance so far! Now that I knew what men were made of, I had confidence that I could save myself from them. The chair, ah, that was different. That was more paralysing than other instruments of torture. But here where I'm lying, the headmaster's room, there are chairs, much bigger and more forbidding than what Captain used to wield, but they have done nothing, they have not moved to menace or hurt me. They have stayed put. Now I've learnt much about chairs and men and the world in general. Perhaps these men were planning to trap me, cage me and force me to continue those jumping turns with the suspended lamb, shamelessly standing on my hind legs before the crowd of film-makers. If this was going to be the case, I must show them that I could be vicious and violent too. So far I had shown great concern and self-control. Thus far and no further. The evidence of my intentions should be the headmaster, who I hoped was somewhere above me, unharmed and, as I hoped, peacefully sleeping. I couldn't be definite. He made no sort of sound or movement, hence I guessed he must be sound asleep. I didn't want to be disturbed, nor was I going to let anyone bother the headmaster. So I had a double responsibility now. Someone at the door. I held myself ready to spring forward.

The door opened quietly and my master entered, shutting the door behind him. I dashed forward to kill the intruder, but I only hurt myself in hurling against the door. I fell back. He was not there, though a moment ago I had seen him enter. I just heard him say, 'Understand that you are not a tiger, don't hurt yourself. I am your friend . . .' How I was beginning to understand his speech was a mystery. He was exercising some strange power over me. His presence sapped all my strength. When I made one more attempt to spring up, I could not raise myself. When he touched me, I tried to hit him, but my forepaw had no strength and collapsed like a rag. When I tried to snap my jaws, again I bit only the air. He merely said, 'Leave that style out. You won't have use for such violent gestures any more. It all goes into your past.' I had to become subdued, having no alternative, while he went on talking. 'It's a natural condition of existence. Every creature is born with a potential store of violence. A child, even before learning to walk, with a pat of its chubby hands just crushes the life out of a tiny ant crawling near it. And as he grows all through life he maintains a vast store of aggressiveness, which will be subdued if he is civilized, or expended in some manner that brings retaliation. But violence cannot be everlasting. Sooner or later it has to go, if not through wisdom, definitely through decrepitude, which comes on with years, whether one wants it or not. The demon, the tormentor, or the tyrant in history, if he ever survives to experience senility, becomes helpless and dependent, lacking the strength even to swat a fly. You are now an adult, full-grown tiger, and assuming you are fifteen years old, in human terms you would be over seventy years old, and at seventy and onwards one's temper gets toned down through normal decay, and let us be grateful for it. You cannot continue your ferocity for ever. You have to change . . .'

At this point someone from the other side of the door called, 'Sir, swamiji, are you all right?'

'Yes, I am, don't you hear me talking?'

'Whom are you talking to, sir?'

'To a friendly soul,' he said.

'Do you mean the headmaster? Is he safe?'

'Yes, he is up there, but I've not begun to talk to him yet . . . he doesn't seem to be awake yet. I'll look to him presently. But at the moment I'm discoursing to the tiger . . .'

'Oh, oh, does it understand?'

'Why not? If you could follow what I've been saying, the tiger should understand me even better since I'm closer to his ear . . .' I let out a roar because I was feeling uncomfortable with some change coming inside me. I was beginning to understand. Don't ask me how. My master never explained to me the mystery or the process of his influence on me.

'Don't let him out, sir,' said the voice. 'When you open the door, please warn us first . . .'

'Surely, if you are afraid, but let me tell you, you need not fear; he has only the appearance of a tiger, but he is not one—inside he is no different from you and me.' I felt restless and wanted to do something or at least get away from the whole situation, back to my familiar life, back to the jungle, to the bed of long grass—I sighed for the feel of the grass on my belly— to the cool of the stream beside the cave and the shade of the cave with its rugged sandy floor . . . I was sick of human beings; they were everywhere, every inch of the earth seemed to be swarming with humanity; ever since the unfortunate day I stepped into that village in the forest to the present moment I was being hemmed in. How grand it'd be to be back in the world of bamboo shade and monkeys and jackals! Even the supercilious leopard and the owl I would not mind; compared to human company, they were pleasant, minding their own business, in spite of occasional moods to taunt and gossip.

I rose. My master became alert. 'What do you want to do now? You want to go away, I suppose! I understand. But there is no going back to your old life, even if I open the door and let you out. You can't go far. You will hurt others or you will surely be hurt. A change is coming, you will have to start a new life, a different one ... Now lie down in peace, I will take you out. Let us go out together, it'll be safer. But first I must get the headmaster down from his perch. He has been there too long. Now you lie still, move away to the corner over there while I help him.'

I understood and slowly moved off to the side he indicated. Whatever its disadvantage, circus life had accustomed me to understand commands. This room was not too spacious to talk of far side and near side, but I obeyed him. I moved to the other wall and crouched there humbly. I wanted to show that I had no aggressive intentions. Now my master ordered, 'Turn your face to the wall and do not stir in the least. If the headmaster thinks you are lifeless, so much the better. The situation is delicate, and you must do nothing to worsen it. God knows how long he has been cooped up there . . .'

He called him loudly but there was no answer. Then he went up to the door, opened it slightly and announced, 'I want a ladder and a person to climb to the loft, wake up the headmaster, and help him to come down. Is there anyone among you willing to fetch the ladder and go up?' A subdued discussion arose and a couple of men came forward to ask, 'What about the tiger? Where is he?'

'You have all improved to the extent of not referring to him as "brute" or "beast", but I'm sorry to note that you still have no confidence in him or me. Let me assure you that this tiger will harm no one.' This had no effect on anyone. There was no response. He said, 'All right, I'll manage . . .' He shut the door again, pulled the table into position, and put up a chair on it, then another chair and a stool, and went up step by step and reached the loft, saying to himself, 'How the headmaster reached here will remain a mystery . . .' He grasped the edge of the loft and heaved himself up.

Presently I heard him waking the headmaster and coaxing him to climb down. I could not see his actual coming down as I had to lie facing the wall; I could only hear movements and words. My master exerted all his power to persuade him to step down. I sensed what was happening and though curious to watch, did not turn round, as I did not want to disobey my master. The first thing the headmaster did on coming down was to cry, 'Oh, it's still here!' and I heard some scurrying of feet, and my master saying, 'Don't look at him, but step down; he will not attack.' The headmaster groaned and whimpered and was possibly trying to go back to the loft, at which my master must have toppled the pile of chairs and pulled him down. I heard a thud and guessed that the poor man had landed on firm ground. I could hear him moaning, 'It is still there, how can I?' My master kept advising, 'What if it is still there? Don't look in its direction, turn away your head, come with me . . .' He led the headmaster as he kept protesting, a sorry spectacle, in disarray, still in the coat and turban which he had worn in the morning. My master propelled him to the door and pushed him out saying to those outside, 'Here he is, take care of him. Not a scratch, only shock . . .' and shut the door again as a medley of comments, questions, and exclamations poured into the room.

Now he addressed me. 'Now turn round, get up, and do whatever you like.' I stretched myself, yawned, and rose to my feet. That was all I could do. I felt grateful, but I could not make out his form clearly. There was a haze in which he seemed to exist, a haze that persisted all through our association. At no time could I be certain of his outline or features—except what I could gather from his talk. He said, 'Let us go out now. You must realize that human beings for all their bluster are timid creatures, and are likely to get into a panic when they see you. But don't look at them. This is one of the rules of yoga: to steady one's mind, to look down one's nose and at nothing beyond. That's one way not to be distracted and to maintain one's peace of mind. I would ask you to keep your head bowed and cast your eyes down and make no sort of sound, whatever may be the reaction of the people we pass. We are bound to meet crowds during our passage through the town. People are likely to get excited at the sight of us, but you must notice nothing.'

This was a necessary instruction since our emergence from the room created a sensation and a stampede, in spite of the warning cry my master had given: 'Now I am coming out with the tiger. Those who are afraid, keep away, but I assure you again that Raja will not attack anyone. He will walk past you, and you will be quite safe as if a cat passed by. Believe me. Otherwise keep out of the way. I'll give you a little time to decide.' When he opened the door, he said, 'Keep close to me.' As he stepped out of the room, I was at his heels, saw no one, but only heard suppressed, excited comments and whispers from different corners. The veranda was empty, not a soul in sight, with the exception of Alphonse lying on the top step. Without a word my master walked on briskly. We had to brush past Alphonse. The breeze of our movement seemed to have blown on his face, and he immediately sat up, rubbed his eyes to see clearly, blinked, shook his head and muttered, 'Crazy dream!' and laid himself down and apparently went back to sleep. But he sat up again to watch us go. We had gone past him a little way when he cried, 'Hey, you bearded one, you again! Won't leave me alone even in a dream! Ah! What is this?'

'Tiger,' answered my master.

'Is it the same or another one?' asked Alphonse.

'Same and another,' answered my master cryptically.

'How? Oh, yes, of course,' he muttered, puzzled.

'You may touch the tiger if you like.'

'No, no! Go away.' He waved us off angrily and resumed his sleep.

THE TRAIN COMES TO MALGUDI

[Narayan's Sahitya Akademi Award-winning novel
The Guide chronicles the story of Raju, a guide who
shows people around Malgudi. The following excerpt
tells of Raju's childhood days and the building of the
railway station at Malgudi, which leads to his taking
up the profession of a guide.]

WE NOTICED MUCH activity in the field in front of
our house. A set of men arrived from the town every
morning and were busy in the field all day. We learned
that they were building a railway track. They came to
my father's shop for refreshments. My father inquired
anxiously, 'When shall we have the trains coming in
here?'

If they were in a good mood, they answered,
'About six or eight months, who can say.' Or if they
were in a black mood, 'Don't ask us. Next you will tell
us to drive a locomotive to your shop!' And they
laughed grimly.

Work was going on briskly. I lost to some extent my freedom under the tamarind tree, because trucks were parked there. I climbed into them and played. No one minded me. All day I was climbing in and out of the trucks, and my clothes became red with mud. Most of the trucks brought red earth which was banked up on the field. In a short while, a small mountain was raised in front of our house. It was enchanting. When I stood on the top of this mound I could see far-off places, the hazy outlines of Mempi Hills. I became as busy as the men. I spent all my time in the company of those working on the track, listening to their talk and sharing their jokes. More trucks came, bringing timber and iron. A variety of goods was piling up on every side. Presently I began to collect sawn-off metal bits, nuts and bolts, and I treasured them in my mother's big trunk, where a space was allotted to me amidst her ancient silk sarees, which she never wore.

A boy grazing his cows approached the spot just below the mound on which I was playing a game by myself. His cows were munching the grass right below the mound on which the men were working, and the little fellow had dared to step on the slope where I played. I was beginning to have a sense of ownership of the railway, and I didn't want trespassers there. I frowned at the boy and barked, 'Get out.'

'Why?' he asked. 'My cows are here, I'm watching them.'

'Begone with your cows,' I said. 'Otherwise they will be run over by the train, which will be here shortly.'

'Let them be. What do you care?' he said, which irritated me so much that I let out a yell and pounced on him with 'You son of a . . .' and a variety of other expressions recently picked up. The boy, instead of knocking me down, ran screaming to my father, 'Your son is using bad language.'

My father sprang up on hearing this. Just my misfortune. He came rushing toward me as I was resuming my game and asked, 'What did you call this boy?' I had the good sense not to repeat it. I blinked, wordlessly, at which the boy repeated exactly what I had said. This produced an unexpectedly violent effect on my father. He grabbed my neck within the hollow of his hand, and asked, 'Where did you pick that up?' I pointed at the men working on the track. He looked up, remained silent for a second, and said, 'Oh, that is so, is it? You will not idle about picking up bad words any more. I will see to it. You will go to a school tomorrow and every day.'

'Father!' I cried. He was passing a harsh sentence on me. To be removed from a place I loved, to a place I loathed!

*

193

One fine day, beyond the tamarind tree, the station building was ready. The steel tracks gleamed in the sun; the signal posts stood with their red and green stripes and their colourful lamps; and our world was neatly divided into this side of the railway line and that side. Everything was ready. All our spare hours were spent in walking along the railway track up to the culvert half a mile away. We paced up and down our platform. A gold mohur sapling was planted in the railway yard. We passed through the corridor, peeping into the room meant for the station master.

One day we were all given a holiday. 'The train comes to our town today,' people said excitedly. The station was decorated with festoons and bunting. A piper was playing, bands were banging away. Coconuts were broken on the railway track, and an engine steamed in, pulling a couple of cars. Many of the important folk of the town were there. The collector and the police superintendent and the municipal chairman, and many of the local tradesmen, who flourished green invitation cards in their hands, were assembled at the station. The police guarded the platform and did not allow the crowds in. I felt cheated by this. I felt indignant that anyone should prohibit my entry to the platform. I squeezed myself through the railings at the farthest end, and by the time the engine arrived I was there to receive it. I was probably so small that no one noticed my presence.

Tables were laid and official gentlemen sat around refreshing themselves, and then several men got up and lectured. I was aware only of the word 'Malgudi' recurring in their speeches. There was a clapping of hands. The band struck up, the engine whistled, the bell rang, the guard blew his whistle, and the men who had been consuming refreshments climbed into the train. I was half inclined to follow their example, but there were many policemen to stop me. The train moved and was soon out of sight. A big crowd was now allowed to come on to the platform. My father's shop had record sales that day.

By the time a station master and a porter were installed in their little stone house at the back of the station, facing our house, my father had become so prosperous that he acquired a jutka and a horse in order to go to the town and do his shopping.

My mother had been apathetic. 'Why should you have all this additional bother in this household, horse and horse-gram and all that, while the buffalo pair is a sufficient bother?'

He did not answer her in any detail, just swept off her objections with, 'You know nothing about these things, I have so much to do every day in the town. I have to visit the bank so often.' He uttered the word 'bank' with a proud emphasis, but it did not impress my mother.

And so there was an addition of a thatch-roofed shed to our yard, in which a brown pony was tied up, and my father had picked up a groom to look after it. We became the talk of the town with this horse and carriage, but my mother never reconciled herself to it. She viewed it as an extraordinary vanity on my father's part and no amount of explanation from him ever convinced her otherwise. Her view was that my father had overestimated his business, and she nagged him whenever he was found at home and the horse and carriage were not put to proper use. She expected him to be always going round the streets in his vehicle. He had not more than an hour's job any day in the town and he always came back in time to attend to his shop, which he was now leaving in charge of a friend for a few hours in the day. My mother was developing into a successful nagger, I suppose, for my father was losing much of his aggressiveness and was becoming very apologetic about his return home whenever the horse and the carriage were left unused under the tamarind tree. 'You take it and go to the market, if you like,' he often said, but my mother spurned the offer, explaining, 'Where should I go every day? Some day it may be useful for going to the temple on a Friday. But ought you to maintain an extravagant turnout all through the year, just for a possible visit to the temple? Horse-gram and grass, do you know what they cost?'

Fortunately, it did not prove such a liability after all. Worn out by Mother's persistent opposition, my father seriously considered disposing of the horse and (a fantastic proposal) converting the carriage into a single bullock-cart with a 'bow spring' mounted over the wheel, which a blacksmith of his acquaintance at the market gate had promised to do for him.

The groom who minded the horse laughed at the idea and said that it was an impossible proposition, convincing my father that the blacksmith would reduce the carriage to a piece of furniture fit for lounging under the tamarind tree. 'You could as well listen to a promise to turn the horse into a bullock!' he said, and then he made a proposal which appealed to my father's business instinct. 'Let me ply it for hire in the market. All gram and grass my charge—only let me use your shed. I will hand you two rupees a day and one rupee a month for the use of the shed, and anything I earn over two rupees should be mine.'

This was a delightful solution. My father had the use of the carriage whenever he wanted it, and earned a sum for it each day, and no liabilities. As the days passed, the driver came along and pleaded lack of engagements. A great deal of argument went on in the front part of my house, in semi-darkness, between my father and the driver as my father tried to exact his two rupees. Finally my mother too joined in, saying,

'Don't trust these fellows. Today with all that festival crowd, he says he has not made any money. How can we believe him?'

My mother was convinced that the cart-driver drank his earnings. My father retorted, 'What if he drinks? It is none of our business.'

Every day this went on. At night the man stood under the tree and cringed and begged for remission. It was evident that he was misappropriating our funds. For within a few weeks the man came and said, 'This horse is growing bony and will not run properly, and is becoming wrong-headed. It is better we sell it off soon and take another, because all the passengers who get into this jutka complain and pay less at the end because of the discomfort suffered. And the springs over the wheels must also be changed.' The man was constantly suggesting that the turnout had better be sold off and a new one taken. Whenever he said it within my mother's hearing she lost her temper and shouted at him, saying that one horse and carriage were sufficient expense. This reduced my father to viewing the whole arrangement as a hopeless liability, until the man hinted that he had an offer of seventy rupees for both horse and carriage. My father managed to raise this to seventy-five and finally the man brought the cash and drove off the turnout himself. Evidently he had saved a lot of our own money for this enterprise. Anyway, we were glad to be rid of the thing. This was a nicely calculated transaction, for as soon as the trains began to arrive regularly at our station we found our jutka doing a brisk business carrying passengers to the town.

My father was given the privilege of running a shop at the railway station. What a shop it was! It was paved with cement, with shelves built in. It was so spacious that when my father had transferred all the articles from the hut-shop, the place was only one-quarter filled; there were so many blank spaces all along the wall that he felt depressed at the sight of it. For the first time he was beginning to feel that he had not been running a very big business after all.

My mother had come out to watch the operation and taunted him, 'With this stock you think of buying motor cars and what not.' He had not at any time proposed buying a motor car but she liked to nag him.

Father said, rather weakly, 'Why drag in all that now?' He was ruminating. 'I shall need at least another five hundred rupees' worth of articles to fill up all this space.'

The station master, an old man wearing a green turban round his head and silver-rimmed spectacles, came along to survey the shop. My father became extremely deferential at the sight of him. Behind him stood Karia the porter in his blue shirt and turban. My mother withdrew unobtrusively and went back home. The station master viewed the shop from a distance with his head on one side as if he were an artist viewing a handiwork. The porter, ever faithful, followed his example, keeping himself in readiness to agree with whatever he might say. The station master said, 'Fill up all that space, otherwise the ATS might come round and ask questions, poking his nose into all our affairs. It has not been easy to give you this shop.'

My father sat me in the shop and went over to the town to make the purchases. 'Don't display too much rice and other stuff—keep the other shop for such things,' advised the station master. 'Railway passengers won't be asking for tamarind and lentils during the journey.' My father implicitly accepted his directions. The station master was his palpable God now and he cheerfully obeyed all his commands. And so, presently there hung down from nails in my father's other shop bigger bunches of bananas, stacks of Mempi oranges, huge troughs of fried stuff, and colourful peppermints and sweets in glass containers, loaves of bread, and buns. The display was most appetizing, and he had loaded several racks with packets of cigarettes. He had to anticipate the demand of every kind of traveller and provide for it.

He left me in charge of his hut-shop. His old customers came down to gossip and shop, as had been their habit. But they found me unequal to it. I found it tedious to listen to their talk of litigation and irrigation. I was not old enough to appreciate all their problems and the subtleties of their transactions. I listened to them without response, and soon they discovered that I was no good as a companion for them. They left me in peace and wandered off to the other shop, seeking my father's company. But they found it untenable. They felt strange there. It was too sophisticated a surrounding for them. Very soon, unobtrusively, my father was back in his seat at the hut-shop, leaving me to handle the business in the new shop. As soon as a certain bridge off Malgudi was ready, regular service began on our rails; it was thrilling to watch the activities of the station master and the blue-shirted porter as they 'received' and 'line-cleared' two whole trains each day, the noon train from Madras and the evening one from Trichy. I became very active indeed in the shop. As you might have guessed, all this business expansion in our family helped me achieve a very desirable end— the dropping off from my school unobtrusively.

A COBRA FOR A COMPANION

[This short story, originally titled 'Naga', is a fascinating tale of a little boy and his pet snake.]

THE BOY TOOK off the lid of the circular wicker basket and stood looking at the cobra coiled inside, and then said, 'Naga, I hope you are dead, so that I may sell your skin to the pursemakers; at least that way you may become useful.' He poked it with a finger. Naga raised its head and looked about with a dull wonder. 'You have become too lazy even to open your hood. You are no cobra. You are an earthworm. I am a snake charmer attempting to show you off and make a living. No wonder so often I have to stand at the bus stop pretending to be blind and beg. The trouble is, no one wants to see you, no one has any respect for you and no one is afraid of you, and do you know what that means? I starve, that is all.'

Whenever the boy appeared at the street door,

householders shooed him away. He had seen his father operate under similar conditions. His father would climb the steps of the house unmindful of the discouragement, settle down with his basket and go through his act heedless of what anyone said. He would pull out his gourd pipe from the bag and play the snake tune over and over, until its shrill, ear-piercing note induced a torpor and made people listen to his preamble: 'In my dream, God Shiva appeared and said, "Go forth and thrust your hand into that crevice in the floor of my sanctum." As you all know, Shiva is the Lord of Cobras, which He ties His braid with, and its hood canopies His head; the great God Vishnu rests in the coils of Adi-Shesha, the mightiest serpent who also bears on his thousand heads this Universe. Think of the armlets on Goddess Parvati! Again, elegant little snakes. How can we think that we are wiser than our gods? Snake is a part of a god's ornament, and not an ordinary creature. I obeyed Shiva's command—at midnight I walked out and put my arm into the snake hole.'

At this point his audience would shudder and someone would ask, 'Were you bitten?'

'Of course I was bitten, but still you see me here, because the same god commanded, "Find that weed growing on the old fort wall." No, I am not going to mention its name, even if I am offered a handful of sovereigns.'

'What did you do with the weed?'

'I chewed it; thereafter no venom could enter my system. And the terrible fellow inside this basket plunged his fangs into my arms like a baby biting his mother's nipple, but I laughed and pulled him out, and knocked off with a piece of stone the fangs that made him so arrogant; and then he understood that I was only a friend and well-wisher, and no trouble after that. After all, what is a serpent? A great soul in a state of penance waiting to go back to its heavenly world. That is all, sirs.'

After this speech, his father would flick open the basket lid and play the pipe again, whereupon the snake would dart up like spring-work, look about and sway a little; people would be terrified and repelled, but still enthralled. At the end of the performance, they gave him coins and rice, and sometimes an old shirt, too, and occasionally he wangled an egg if he observed a hen around; seizing Naga by the throat, he let the egg slide down its gullet, to the delight of the onlookers. He then packed up and repeated the performance at the next street or at the bazaar, and when he had collected sufficient food and cash he returned to his hut beside the park wall, in the shade of a big tamarind tree. He cooked the rice and fed his son, and they slept outside the hut, under the stars.

*

The boy had followed his father ever since he could walk, and when he attained the age of ten his father let him handle Naga and harangue his audience in his own style. His father often said, 'We must not fail to give Naga two eggs a week. When he grows old, he will grow shorter each day; someday he will grow wings and fly off, and do you know that at that time he will spit out the poison in his fangs in the form of a brilliant jewel, and if you possessed it you could become a king?'

One day when the boy had stayed beside the hut out of laziness, he noticed a tiny monkey gambolling amidst the branches of the tamarind tree and watched it with open-mouthed wonder, not even noticing his father arrive home.

'Boy, what are you looking at? Here, eat this,' said the father, handing him a packet of sweets. 'They gave it to me at that big house, where some festival is going on. Naga danced to the pipe wonderfully today. He now understands all our speech. At the end of his dance, he stood six feet high on the tip of his tail, spread out his hood, hissed and sent a whole crowd scampering. Those people enjoyed it, though, and gave me money and sweets.' His father looked happy as he opened the lid of the basket. The cobra raised its head. His father held it up by the neck, and forced a bit of a sweet between its jaws, and watched it work its way down. 'He is now one of our family and should learn to eat what we eat,' he said. After struggling through the sweet, Naga coiled himself down, and the man clapped the lid back.

The boy munched the sweet with his eyes still fixed on the monkey. 'Father, I wish I were a monkey: I'd never come down from the tree. See how he is nibbling all that tamarind fruit . . . Hey, monkey, get me a fruit!' he cried.

The man was amused, and said, 'This is no way to befriend him. You should give *him* something to eat, not ask him to feed you.'

At which the boy spat out his sweet, wiped it clean with his shirt, held it up and cried, 'Come on, monkey! Here!'

His father said, 'If you call him "monkey", he will never like you. You must give him a nice name.'

'What shall we call him?'

'Rama, name of the master of Hanuman, the Divine Monkey. Monkeys adore that name.'

The boy at once called, 'Rama, here, take this.' He flourished his arms, holding up the sweet, and the monkey did pause in its endless antics and notice him. The boy hugged the tree trunk, and heaved himself up, and carefully placed the sweet on the flat surface of a forking branch, and the monkey watched with round-eyed wonder. The boy slid back to the ground and eagerly waited for the monkey to come down and accept the gift. While he watched and the monkey was debating within himself, a crow appeared from somewhere and took away the sweet. The boy shrieked out a curse.

His father cried, 'Hey, what? Where did you learn this foul word? No monkey will respect you if you utter bad words.' Ultimately, when the little monkey was tempted down with another piece of sweet, his father caught him deftly by the wrist, holding him off firmly by the scruff to prevent his biting.

Fifteen days of starvation, bullying, cajoling and dangling of fruit before the monkey's eyes taught him what he was expected to do. First of all, he ceased trying to bite or scratch. And then he realized that his mission in life was to please his master by performing. At a command from his master, he could demonstrate how Hanuman, the Divine Monkey of the *Ramayana*, strode up and down with tail ablaze and set Ravana's capital on fire; how an oppressed village daughter-in-law would walk home carrying a pitcher of water on her head; how a newly-wed would address his beloved (chatter, blink, raise the brow and grin); and, finally, what was natural to him—tumbling and acrobatics on top of a bamboo pole. When Rama was ready to appear in public, his master took him to a roadside-tailor friend of his and had him measured out for a frilled jacket, leaving the tail out, and a fool's cap held in position with a band under his small chin. Rama constantly tried to push his cap back and rip it off, but whenever he attempted it he was whacked with a switch, and he soon resigned himself to wearing his uniform until the end of the day. When his master stripped off Rama's clothes, the monkey performed spontaneous somersaults in sheer relief.

*

Rama became popular. Schoolchildren screamed with joy at the sight of him. Householders beckoned to him to step in and divert a crying child. He performed competently, earned money for his master and peanuts for himself. Discarded baby clothes were offered to him as gifts. The father-son team started out each day, the boy with the monkey riding on his shoulder and the cobra basket carried by his father at some distance away—for the monkey chattered and shrank, his face disfigured with fright, whenever the cobra hissed and reared itself up. While the young fellow managed to display the tricks of the monkey to a group, he could hear his father's pipe farther off. At the weekly market fairs in the villages around, they were a familiar pair, and they became prosperous enough to take a bus home at the end of the day. Sometimes as they started to get on, a timid passenger would ask, 'What's to happen if the cobra gets out?'

'No danger. The lid is secured with a rope,' the father would reply.

There would always be someone among the passengers to remark, 'A snake minds its business until you step on its tail.'

'But this monkey?' another passenger would say. 'God knows what he will be up to!'

'He is gentle and wise,' the father would say, and he'd offer a small tip to win the conductor's favour.

They travelled widely, performing at all market fairs, and earned enough money to indulge in an occasional tiffin at a restaurant. The boy's father would part company from him in the evening, saying, 'Stay. I've a stomach ache; I'll get some medicine for it and come back,' and return tottering late at night. The boy felt frightened of his father at such moments, and, lying on his mat, with the monkey tethered to a stake nearby, would pretend to be asleep. Father would kick him and say, 'Get up, lazy swine. Sleeping when your father after slaving for you all day comes home for a chat with you. You are not my son but a bastard.' But the boy would not stir.

*

One night the boy really fell asleep, and woke up in the morning to find his father gone. The monkey was also missing. 'They must have gone off together!' he cried. He paced up and down and called, 'Father!' several times. He then peered into the hut and found the round basket intact in its corner. He noticed on the lid of the basket some coins, and felt rather pleased when he counted them and found eighty paise in small change. 'It must all be for me,' he said to himself. He felt promoted to adulthood, handling so much cash. He felt rich but also puzzled at his father's tactics. Ever since he could remember, he had never woken up without finding his father at his side. He had a foreboding that he was not going to see his father anymore. Father would never at any time go out without announcing his purpose—for a bath at the street tap, or to seek medicine for a 'stomach ache', or to do a little shopping.

The boy lifted the lid of the basket to make sure that the snake at least was there. It popped up the moment the lid was taken off. He looked at it, and it looked at him for a moment. 'I'm your master now. Take care.' As if understanding the changed circumstances, the snake darted its forked tongue and half-opened its hood. He tapped it down with his finger, saying, 'Get back. Not yet.' Would it be any use waiting for his father to turn up? He felt hungry.

Wondered if it'd be proper to buy his breakfast with the coins left on the basket lid. If his father should suddenly come back, he would slap him for taking the money. He put the lid back on the snake, put the coins back on the lid as he had found them and sat at the mouth of the hut, vacantly looking at the tamarind tree and sighing for his monkey, which would have displayed so many fresh and unexpected pranks early in the morning. He reached for a little cloth bag in which was stored a variety of nuts and fried pulses to feed the monkey. He opened the bag, examined the contents and put a handful into his mouth and chewed: 'Tastes so good. Too good for a monkey, but Father will . . .' His father always clouted his head when he caught him eating nuts meant for the monkey. Today he felt free to munch the nuts, although worried at the back of his mind lest his father should suddenly remember and come back for the monkey's food. He found the gourd pipe in its usual place, stuck in the thatch. He snatched it up and blew through its reeds, feeling satisfied that he could play as well as his father and that the public would not know the difference; only it made him cough a little and gasp for breath. The shrill notes attracted the attention of people passing by the hut, mostly day labourers carrying spades and pickaxes and women carrying baskets, who nodded their heads approvingly and remarked, 'True son of the father.'

Everyone had a word with him. All knew him in that colony of huts, which had cropped up around the water fountain. All the efforts of the municipality to dislodge these citizens had proved futile; the huts sprang up as often as they were destroyed, and when the municipal councillors realized the concentration of voting power in this colony, they let the squatters alone, except when some VIP from Delhi passed that way, and then they were asked to stay out of sight, behind the park wall, till the eminent man had flashed past in his car.

'Why are you not out yet?' asked a woman.

'My father is not here,' the boy said pathetically. 'I do not know where he is gone.' He sobbed a little.

The woman put down her basket, sat by his side and asked, 'Are you hungry?'

'I have money,' he said.

She gently patted his head and said, 'Ah, poor child! I knew your mother. She was a good girl. That she should have left you adrift like this and gone heavenward!' Although he had no memory of his mother, at the mention of her, tears rolled down his cheeks, and he licked them off with relish at the corner of his mouth. The woman suddenly said, 'What are you going to do now?'

'I don't know,' he said. 'Wait till my father comes.'

'Foolish and unfortunate child. Your father is gone.'

'Where?' asked the boy.

'Don't ask me,' the woman said. 'I talked to a man who saw him go. He saw him get into the early-morning bus, which goes up the mountains, and that strumpet in the blue saree was with him.'

'What about the monkey?' the boy asked. 'Won't it come back?'

She had no answer to this question. Meanwhile, a man hawking idlis on a wooden tray was crying his wares at the end of the lane. The woman hailed him in a shrill voice and ordered, 'Sell this poor child two idlis. Give him freshly-made ones, not yesterday's.'

'Yesterday's stuff not available even for a gold piece,' said the man.

'Give him the money,' she told the boy. The boy ran in and fetched some money. The woman pleaded with the hawker, 'Give him something extra for the money.'

'What extra?' he snarled.

'This is an unfortunate child.'

'So are others. What can I do? Why don't you sell your earrings and help him? I shall go bankrupt if I listen to people like you and start giving more for less money.' He took the cash and went on. Before he reached the third hut, the boy had polished off the idlis—so soft and pungent, with green chutney spread on top.

The boy felt more at peace with the world now, and able to face his problems. After satisfying herself that he had eaten well, the woman rose to go, muttering, 'Awful strumpet, to seduce a man from his child.' The boy sat and brooded over her words. Though he gave no outward sign of it, he knew who the strumpet in the blue saree was. She lived in one of those houses beyond the park wall and was always to be found standing at the door, and seemed to be a fixture there. At the sight of her, his father would slow down his pace and tell the boy, 'You keep going. I'll join you.' The first time it happened, after waiting at the street corner, the boy tied the monkey to a lamp-post and went back to the house. He did not find either his father or the woman where he had left them. The door of the house was shut. He raised his hand to pound on it, but restrained himself and sat down on the step, wondering. Presently the door opened and his father emerged, with the basket slung over his shoulder as usual; he appeared displeased at the sight of the boy and raised his hand to strike him, muttering, 'Didn't I say, "Keep going"?' The boy ducked and ran down the street, and heard the blue-saree woman remark, 'Bad, mischievous devil, full of evil curiosity!' Later, his father said, 'When I say go, you must obey.'

'What did you do there?' asked the boy, trying to

look and sound innocent, and the man said severely, 'You must not ask questions.'

'Who is she? What is her name?'

'Oh, she is a relative,' the man said. To further probing questions he said, 'I went in to drink tea. You'll be thrashed if you ask more questions, little devil.'

The boy said, as an afterthought, 'I only came back thinking that you might want me to take the basket,' whereupon his father said sternly, 'No more talk. You must know, she is a good and lovely person.' The boy did not accept this description of her. She had called him names. He wanted to shout from the rooftops, 'Bad, bad, and bad woman and not at all lovely!' but kept it to himself. Whenever they passed that way again, the boy quickened his pace, without looking left or right, and waited patiently for his father to join him at the street corner. Occasionally his father followed his example and passed on without glancing at the house if he noticed, in place of the woman, a hairy-chested man standing at the door, massaging his pot-belly.

*

The boy found that he could play the pipe, handle the snake and feed it also—all in the same manner as his father used to. Also, he could knock off the fangs

whenever they started to grow. He earned enough
each day, and as the weeks and months passed he
grew taller, and the snake became progressively tardy
and flabby and hardly stirred its coils. The boy never
ceased to sigh for the monkey. The worst blow his
father had dealt him was the kidnapping of his monkey.

When a number of days passed without any earnings,
he decided to rid himself of the snake, throw away the
gourd pipe and do something else for a living. Perhaps
catch another monkey and train it. He had watched his
father and knew how to go about this. A monkey on
his shoulder would gain him admission anywhere, even
into a palace. Later on, he would just keep it as a pet
and look for some other profession. Start as a porter
at the railway station—so many trains to watch every
hour—and maybe get into one someday and out into
the wide world. But the first step would be to get rid
of Naga. He couldn't afford to find eggs and milk for
him.

He carried the snake basket along to a lonely spot
down the river course, away from human habitation,
where a snake could move about in peace without
getting killed at sight. In that lonely part of Nallappa's
Grove, there were many mounds, crevices and anthills.
'You could make your home anywhere there, and your
cousins will be happy to receive you back into their
fold,' he said to the snake. 'You should learn to be

happy in your own home. You must forget me. You have become useless, and we must part. Don't know where my father has gone. He'd have kept you until you grew wings and all that, but I don't care.' He opened the lid of the basket, lifted the snake and set it free. It lay inert for a while, then raised its head, looked at the outside world without interest, and started to move along tardily, without any aim. After a few yards of slow motion, it turned about, looking for its basket home. At once the boy snatched up the basket and flung it far out of the snake's range. 'You will not go anywhere else as long as I am nearby.' He turned the snake round, to face an anthill, prodded it on and then began to run at full speed in the opposite direction. He stopped at a distance, hid himself behind a tree and watched. The snake was approaching the slope of the anthill. The boy had no doubt now that Naga would find the hole on its top, slip itself in and vanish from his life forever.

The snake crawled halfway up the hill, hesitated and then turned round and came along in his direction again. The boy swore, 'Oh, damned snake! Why don't you go back to your world and stay there? You won't find me again.' He ran through Nallappa's Grove and stopped to regain his breath. From where he stood, he saw his Naga glide along majestically across the ground, shining like a silver ribbon under the bright sun. The boy paused to say 'Goodbye' before making his exit. But looking up he noticed a white-necked Brahmany kite sailing in the blue sky. 'Garuda,' he said in awe. As was the custom, he made obeisance to it by touching his eyes with his fingertips. Garuda was the vehicle of God Vishnu and was sacred. He shut his eyes in a brief prayer to the bird. 'You are a god, but I know you eat snakes. Please leave Naga alone.' He opened his eyes and saw the kite skimming along a little nearer, its shadow almost trailing the course of the lethargic snake. 'Oh!' he screamed. 'I know your purpose.' Garuda would make a swoop and dive at the right moment and stab his claws into that foolish Naga, who had refused the shelter of the anthill, and carry him off for his dinner. The boy dashed back to the snake, retrieving his basket on the way. When he saw the basket, Naga slithered back into it, as if coming home after a strenuous public performance.

Naga was eventually reinstated in his corner at the hut beside the park wall. The boy said to the snake, 'If you don't grow wings soon enough, I hope you will be hit on the head with a bamboo staff, as it normally happens to any cobra. Know this: I will not be guarding you forever. I'll be away at the railway station, and if you come out of the basket and adventure about, it will be your end. No one can blame me afterward.'

A TRYST AT THE TEMPLE

[In this short story, originally titled 'Nitya', a young man makes a trip to a distant temple with his parents to fulfil a vow that he doesn't want to.]

'NITYA, AT SIX on Friday morning,' said his father determinedly, 'we leave by bus.' Nitya had noticed preparations at home for this trip, Mother planning a packed lunch for three and filling a basket with coconut, flowers, and incense for worship at the temple. Nitya knew very well how much he was involved in their plans. His mother had talked of nothing else whenever he stepped into the kitchen for coffee. 'After all, a vow has to be fulfilled,' she would keep repeating. Nitya would try to change the subject, banter, joke about it, and run away. They had made a vow to God in a distant hill that Nitya's head would be shaved clean and his hair offered with due rites if his life was spared. That was when he was two years old and stricken with whooping cough and convulsions. Now he was twenty, and although the time limit for fulfilment seemed to be past, yet, they felt, it would not be safe or proper to postpone further. When casually turning the leaves of an old diary, Father discovered the record of their promise to God. Mother, too, recollected having knotted a little coin in a piece of cloth as a reminder, although she could not trace it now. The promise and the diary were lost sight of during Nitya's growing years when the family suddenly found itself drawn into a legal battle over their property. The case was prolonged year after year through the labours of a specially gifted lawyer on the opposite side who could manoeuvre a postponement out of the toughest judge at a crucial point, with the idea of starting it all over again before a new judge in due course. Father was determined to fight it out as the will was unequivocally in his favour and made him sole heir to the property. By the time the final decision came his assets had dwindled, and his lawyer himself had changed from a scintillating youth of promise to a toothless character in a frayed gown haunting the corridors of the civil court.

Today, when Father mentioned a firm date for the trip, Nitya protested, 'It doesn't concern me, your twenty-year-old promise. You had no business to pawn my scalp without consulting me.'

'You were only two years old then.'

'You should have done it when you could handle my head as you pleased.'

'But you were very sick and for a long time, too.'

'I have survived, which proves that the disease died rather than me and so where is God's hand in this, if there is a God and if He is interested in my hair?'

His parents were aghast at his manner of talk. Mother pleaded, 'Whatever you do, don't talk like that.'

Father admonished, 'Nitya, you must not be blasphemous. If God hadn't responded to our prayers and saved your life ...' He could not complete the sentence.

'Was it a bargain?' Nitya asked leeringly.

'Yes,' replied his father. 'It was indeed a bargain and there can be no going back on it.'

'Very well, but the head offered for a shave was not yours. You have been carrying on negotiations with a commodity that did not belong to you.'

'It was for your welfare.'

'Did I ask for it?' Nitya asked puckishly. His mother burst into tears. Father remarked with a scowl, 'You talk like a sinner, cold and godless. Wonder where you inherited it from.'

At this point their neighbour, an alcoholic who had stationed himself in front of the house listening to their debate, suddenly thundered from the street, 'Silence! I am wifeless. Others have two or three—selfish bastards!' He had been a chief engineer in government service, but was dismissed for drunkenness, and later abandoned by his family, too. Nitya loved his antics as he strode up and down the street shouting obscenities after visits to the tavern at the market. Nitya had noted in his private journal: 'The merry engineer mistook the kitchen for the toilet, and that proved too much for his better half.' Now on the pretext of sending him away, Nitya went down the steps and escaped his parents. Later, however, his father kept a close watch on him and clung to him till they reached their seats in the yellow bus at the market gate on Friday.

Father looked triumphant with Nitya secure at his side in the bus, and engaged him in small talk. Mother sat away from them in a back row, enjoying the company of women returning to their villages. The bus passed through Ellamann Street and crossed Nallappa's Grove and climbed the other bank of the river, splashing up water. The driver displayed immense self-assurance and goaded his bus on with reckless gusto. Passengers were tossed sideways and jolted up and down, but no one minded except Nitya. 'What sort of journey is this?' he asked.

'You must learn to be patient, my boy, ours is a

poor country. We cannot afford the luxuries they have in Bombay or Madras.' The passengers, mostly villagers, were happy chatting and laughing and also exchanging jokes with the conductor from time to time. Passengers got in and out all along the route whenever the bus stopped, with its wheels screeching and churning up dust. At certain points the bus became almost empty, at others overcrowded, the conductor shouting, 'Move up, move up'. People got in somehow and stayed on somehow, packed to the windscreen. No one protested, but parted with their coins cheerfully. The conductor, hanging on the footboard precariously, pocketed all the cash, which inspired Nitya to note in his diary, 'The bus rocks and sways, and sighs with its burden, but won't burst yet. Perhaps the last straw is yet to arrive. But the real question is, Who owns this? Definitely not this conductor, though he grows heavier every minute with the coins dropping like manna into his pocket.'

'You should get down here and walk up to that hill, the bus can't take you there,' said the conductor at a stop. They struggled their way out of the bus, Mother carrying her bundle of offerings and food delicately through the crush. As the bus started on its way again, Father asked the driver, 'When are you returning?'

'At five, six, or seven; if you miss, tomorrow morning.' The temple perched on a hillock was visible across the field, but it was impossible to judge the distance. A track formed by the tread of feet meandered through the fields. They had to cross in single file with Nitya in the middle, Father ahead, and Mother bringing up the rear. Nitya reflected, 'Afraid I might run away, they are sandwiching me. But what chance have I, trapped by slush and vegetation on both sides of this narrow path.'

An hour's walk brought them to a hamlet skirting the base of the hillock. Nitya was on the point of asking, Why come so far, if God is everywhere? I could as well have surrendered my head to our Vinayak Street barber, who shaves you at your doorstep. As if reading his mind, Father began to explain, 'This temple was established by our ancestors 500 years ago; it's on this hill that Kumara annihilated the demon whose name I can't recollect now.'

'Demon is a demon, whatever the name,' said the young man. Father ignored his quip and continued, 'The temple was built by a Chola king who ruled these parts, and in course of time it was turned over to the care of our ancestors.'

'How are you sure?' Nitya asked.

'You've got into the habit of questioning everything.'

'I just want to know, that's all.'

'Well, it is all recorded in copper plates, stone pillars, and palm leaves, from which deductions are made by scholars. Don't imagine you are the only wise

man. There is a document in the temple in palm leaf
mentioning my great-grandfather by name and
committing our family to the expenses of the annual
chariot festival. I pay them Rs 200 a year and twenty
measures of rice for a public feast on that day. They
come to the town for collections in December, ten
days before the festival ... Luckily, a copy of this
document is in my possession with the receipts of
annual payments which clinched the issue in our favour
at the appellate stage.' Nitya noted later in his diary,
'Even at this distance and on a consecrated spot my
father is unable to keep his mind off the civil court,
verily like the engineer of his wifelessness.' When they
came to the border of the village, Father slowed his
steps and, with a slight frown, threw a general question
in the air: 'Where is everybody?' as if the reception
committee had failed him.

He halted at a corner and shouted, 'Hey, Rama,'
and a group of women and boys emerged from some
corner and came running on seeing him. They invited
him into their homes. Father said impatiently, 'Yes,
later. First the temple. Call the headman.'

'They are all away weeding,' said a woman, and
turning to a young man jabbed his cheek with her
forefinger and said, 'Run up and tell Rama that the
trustee has come.' The boy shot off like an arrow.
They dragged out of their homes an assortment of

furniture and put it up in the shade of a tree, and then bustled about and conjured up a bunch of bananas and a jug of milk for the visitors and laid the fare on a wooden stool. Nitya cried, 'Oh, just what I need,' and tried to reach out for a fruit, but Father said, 'Not now, after the vow.' (Nitya noted in his diary, 'Not now, but after the vow, says God through my father in a perfect rhyme, while the banana wilts in the tray and the milk curdles irreparably.') The headman arrived. After the initial courtesies, much business talk ensued, with a crowd standing around and listening intently. Father inquired authoritatively, 'Where is the priest? The temple must be opened. We have to leave by the evening bus.'

The headman said out of courtesy, 'Must you? You may spend the night at the rest house, sir. You have come after a long time.'

Immediately, Nitya protested, 'You may both stay back if you choose, but I want to catch the bus,' feeling nostalgic for his evening group at the College Union. Mother said, 'Be patient.' But Nitya replied, 'I've much to do this evening.' Father said, 'What could be more important than your duty to God? Be patient, having come so far.'

The temple priest, his forehead ablaze with sacred ash and vermilion, shoulders wrapped in a red shawl, a lanky person with a booming voice, arrived, dangling a large key in an iron hoop. After greeting the trustee in the correct manner, he plunged straight into business, cataloguing his demands.

'The well at the temple needs to be deepened. The temple lock must be replaced. It is worn out, sir. These are very bad days. We are finding it difficult to get flowers for the worship. We were getting supplies from the other village. But they raise their rates each time and are very irregular too. They have to come up from the other side of the hill and don't like it, and so have started a rumour that they see a wolf or panther prowling around, and have stopped coming altogether.'

'Nonsense, only an excuse,' cried Father. 'No panther or tiger in these parts, never heard such rubbish in my life.'

'He mentioned wolf, not tiger,' corrected Nitya.

'What if he did? It is just gossip and nonsense—rumour-mongers!' Father cried with passion, looking outraged at the notion of any wild-life in the vicinity of his ancestral temple. He dismissed the subject peremptorily and commanded, 'Get the barber down. My son's tonsure must be done today whatever happens,' and the assembly looked with fresh interest at Nitya's head, at which he simpered, squirmed, and ran his fingers through his crop. The priest turned to a little fellow in the crowd and said, 'Don't bite your nail, you fool! Go to the tank bund and tell Raghavan to come up with his tin box immediately, this very second. Run, run.' The little messenger was off like a shot again.

They started up the hill, led by the priest, a crowd following. It was a short climb, but Nitya's mother panted and rested in three places, while Father hovered around her and fidgeted impatiently. The climb ended at the door of the temple, which was unlocked, and two large doors were pushed open. It was a little shrine with a granite-pillared hall and paved corridor around the sanctum, which housed an image on a pedestal. Father became grim and devout. Mother shut her eyes and recited a prayer. The priest lit the wicks in the sanctum and the image began to glow with the oil anointed on it and gradually took shape. The priest was grumbling, 'Even this oil is adulterated nowadays.' He had managed to secure a handful of marigolds and nerium and stuck them on the image. While they were all in this state of elation, the young messenger returned from his mission and bellowed from the door, 'The barber's house is locked, not a soul there.'

'Did you ask the neighbours?'

'They don't know. They only saw the family go out for the bus with their baggage.'

Nitya cried aloud, 'God is great, really.'

Father commented, 'This is the worst of it, having one barber for the whole place. He thinks he can do what he pleases. One and only Padmavathi for a whole city, as the saying goes,' he said, unable to contain himself. His wife said with a frown, 'Hush! What awful words to utter in this place.' Father glowered at her for checking him, but they were all assembled in the presence of God and could not engage in acrimony. Nitya giggled but suppressed himself when his father glanced in his direction. The headman said in a respectful whisper, 'Raghavan cannot make both ends meet unless he ekes out with the fee for playing the pipe at weddings. It is their family tradition.' Father leaned over to Mother and whispered, 'For thousands of years somehow barbers have also been outstanding pipers and custodians of pure classical music.' While this was going on, the priest sounded a bell and circled a camphor flame around the image and they stopped talking and were lost in meditation.

When the priest came out of the sanctum, bearing a tray with a camphor flame, a discussion began as to what course of action the scriptures prescribed when an essential barber was absent.

'We are at the mercy of a single man,' Father kept repeating monotonously, firmly suppressing the name 'Padmavathi', which kept bobbing up again and again on his tongue. The priest put the tray back in the sanctum, came out, and joined the discussion. He finally said, gaping at Nitya's crop, which was the main topic of discussion and purpose of the trip, 'Sometimes, the vow is taken to be fulfilled through a token performance with penalty added. These days young men will not allow barbers to come near them.'

'They won't allow their terrifying whiskers to be touched either!' added Father.

'No tonsure is possible unless done in babyhood,' said the priest.

'Too true, well spoken,' said Nitya, pleased with the tenor of talks, and offered, 'Get me a pair of scissors, and I will give you four inches of my front lock, the best available—that's all, and God will be satisfied. After all, with so many offerings, where can he keep his collection?'

The priest said, 'The fruits and coconuts you have brought are adequate, leave them behind, and add whatever cash you can spare.'

Father and Mother looked disappointed and kept throwing covetous glances at Nitya's head. Nitya felt relieved, but the relief threatened to be short-lived. Soon there was a commotion. Someone at the doorway announced excitedly, 'Raghavan is coming up,' followed by the appearance of a fat barber holding in his hand a tiny tin box. He was panting and perspiring; he stared at the gathering from the doorway, and without a word went straight to the well at the backyard, peeled off his vest, drew a pot of water and emptied it over his head, and reappeared, dripping and ready. 'He never opens his razor box without a bath at first when he has to perform a tonsure ceremony,' explained the priest admiringly. The barber explained, 'I had only gone to a nearby farm for a baby's first shave, that was all.'

'Not to play the pipe at a wedding?' someone asked.

'Oh, no. I have jealous neighbours who create false rumours to spoil my business. If I had known the trustee was coming I would not have accepted even a thousand pieces of gold anywhere outside. When the boy came on a bicycle and told me, I snatched it from his hand and rode down immediately. Now I am ready, my master.' Father and Mother looked pleased at this turn of events. Nitya giggled at the thought of the fat barber on the boy's bicycle. Father took Nitya by hand. 'Let us sit on that stone platform in the corridor, that's where he shaves—'

Nitya shook himself free and said, 'I agreed to give four inches of hair, it was up to you to have taken it. Now you have lost the opportunity, which must be seized by the forelock.'

'Now, with this man here, we must fulfil the vow as originally promised,' said Mother.

'Let Father use the barber if he likes. I'm not interested.'

The barber started pleading and arguing. The priest edged up to Nitya with his pleas and said ingratiatingly, 'You must not hurt your parents' feelings. Please move on to that platform, the barber is ready.'

'But my head is not ready. You promised to accept four inches of my hair. Now you are demanding my head itself. Have you no logic or reason? No contentment or consistency? How can God tolerate fickle-minded people like you! Now I have changed my mind—I won't give even an inch . . .'

Both Father and Mother cried simultaneously, 'Don't talk to the priest like that in his own temple.' Nitya was angry, also hungry. They would not let him touch even one plantain out of the dozens offered by the villagers under the tree. While his parents stood staring at him helplessly, Nitya suddenly turned on his heel, dashed out, and sped downhill saying, 'I will wait for you both at the bus stop, but only till the bus arrives . . .'

TIM ARRIVES IN KABIR STREET

[In Narayan's last novel, The World of Nagaraj, *the ageing Nagaraj's world of small comforts and his contemplation of the epic on Narada that he plans to write are rudely interrupted by the arrival of his young nephew Tim. The following excerpt is about Tim's sudden appearance in Malgudi, and the drama that this sets into motion.]*

ON THE FEW occasions when Nagaraj visited his brother at the village, he noticed his nephew Tim going to a 'pyol school'—that was a sort of mud platform canopied with thatch and straw and presided over by the local pedagogue who conducted his classes by shouting and flourishing his cane at the children who squatted before him. This teaching method was much appreciated by the village elders, who based their educational philosophy on the proverb, 'The unbeaten child will remain unlearned'. Nagaraj felt sickened: a far cry from St Stephen's in Malgudi, which was a coveted school where Tim was admitted by Nagaraj when the brothers lived together in Kabir Street as an undivided family; and definitely worse than the derelict municipal school in which he and his brother had studied as children. He did not talk about it for fear of irritating Gopu. Luckily the shed collapsed during a storm, and the platform was washed off; the pedagogue could not rebuild it.

Thus ended the educational career of the village children, who turned to performing odd tasks on their farms. Gopu, however, sent Tim to a town school five miles away. The boy had to walk a mile to catch a highway bus after waiting for it under an avenue tree. It was tedious. Some days, if the bus arrived late, he missed it deliberately, since he did not like to be caned for going late to his class. So he just dawdled and wandered about and marked time till he could go back home. Some days, if a bus going in the direction of Malgudi came up, he jumped into it and secretly visited his uncle at Kabir Street. He enjoyed his visits to his uncle as he was received with warmth and feted in their house. Nagaraj saved the boy embarrassment by not questioning him too closely about his movements but took care to return him to his village in the evening bus.

It was a busy hour at the Saree Centre, which

meant the noisiest moment with customers, all women, discussing the worth of various types and patterns and their suitability for occasions. Nagaraj was quite used to this din. He could go on with his accounting and entries without feeling disturbed. He sat in his corner bent over his papers, and did not hear the call from across his table, 'Uncle! I've come—' When he looked up he saw Tim standing before him. He almost rubbed his eyes to be sure that it was no apparition.

'Tim! Why did you not tell me you were coming?' Nagaraj put away his books, wiped the pen with the rag which was always in its place on his desk under a glass paperweight. He locked up the ledgers, murmured to Tim again, 'Sit down on that stool. I'll be with you in a minute.'

Nagaraj sensed that this was unlike other visits by Tim. The boy, who usually looked bright and happy during his visits, now looked glum and only muttered, when questioned, 'I've come away with my trunk.' What was the significance of the mention of the trunk? Nagaraj suspected some complication back at the village and only said, 'Wait, sit on that stool. I'll be with you soon.' In a little while he went to Coomar, said something, and joined his nephew.

'Let's go,' he said. The boy stood up and gazed with wonder at the crowd of women and the colourful sarees spread on the mat. Carrying his small trunk,

Tim accompanied Nagaraj home. They walked silently. Nagaraj was afraid to open his mouth lest some impossible situation should reveal itself.

Sita, opening the door, was surprised to see Tim. Nagaraj said inanely, 'He has come with his trunk.' While he went in to change and wash, she took charge of Tim and his trunk, and gave him coffee and tiffin, and decided not to question him. Nagaraj's mother was in a far corner of the house in the second courtyard, on her routine wandering, and was not yet aware of her grandson's arrival.

When Nagaraj was ready for a talk, he felt a little anxious and nervous. He seated Tim on the pyol and asked, 'Now, tell me what happened. Why are you carrying your trunk?'

'Because I am not going back—'

'Oh!' exclaimed Nagaraj, rather pleased. 'Surely . . . But does your father know?'

'He should know, he saw me walking out with the trunk.'

Nagaraj realized that the boy attached some extraordinary significance to the trunk. He remained silent; some neighbours passing down the street noticed them conversing and slowed down their pace, hoping to overhear their talk. The executive engineer of the last house, returning from the bar, cried on seeing Tim, 'Hello! How you have grown, like the eucalyptus tree which stood around my office in the hills. Say namaste to your elders,' and passed on.

Tim volunteered to explain, 'He called me a donkey—'

'Who?'

'Father.'

'Why?' Nagaraj asked aloud, but added within, 'Why not?'

The boy explained, 'He asked me to go to the fields and report to him on the work people were doing. I hesitated, I had to go out to catch the bus, otherwise I would be punished for going late. He called me "donkey". I said, "What's a donkey, Father?" and he slapped my face. My mother was away.'

'Otherwise what would have happened?' Nagaraj asked, his curiosity stirred as to how Charu would confront her husband. He asked, 'Does your mother . . .?' He could not find the right word. He swallowed back the phrase, 'Quarrel with him?' It would have been very pleasing to hear that she did, but he changed his sentence to 'Did she tell you what to do?'

The boy was rather puzzled at the nature of the enquiry, and said, 'I packed up my trunk and left. Mother was returning just as I was leaving. I met her on the way and told her, "I'm going to Malgudi and will not be back." She asked many questions but I could not answer them. She tried to hold me back and snatched away my trunk but I shook myself free and ran, crying, "I won't come back. Don't wait . . ." '

Nagaraj felt confused by this muddled account and said, 'Stay here by all means. I'll be happy . . .' He felt his brother was likely to turn up sooner or later and worsen the situation. He felt a terrible responsibility had fallen on him.

Nagaraj was sitting on the pyol, spending the evening as usual looking at the coconut trees with crows retiring for the night. Before repairing to the trees they assembled on the roof of the tall house in the opposite row. Scores of them flew down and perched like schoolchildren under the supervision of a convent sister. The crows argued a lot among themselves and hopped and shifted about before dispersing. Nagaraj always felt a fascination for this evening activity of the crows, and wished he knew the language of birds as did the kings of folklore. The crows probably had a leader who alloted them treetops for the night and they argued and debated about it before coming to a decision. The leader would probably be saying, 'Don't you see the sky is reddening? Hurry up, darkness will soon be upon us, and remember we are not human beings who light lamps for their night life . . .'

This fantasy was shattered when a jutka halted in

front of him, wheels crunching the gravel. He could not believe his eyes: his brother emerged from the jutka. As he stepped down, all the pent-up affection in Nagaraj burst forth, 'Oh, Gopu, come, come. Why didn't you write to me you were coming? I'd have met you at the bus stand—you came by bus?'

'How else? Did you expect me to come in an aeroplane from our village?'

'Why not? Within ten years you may have plane service all over . . .'

'Don't talk nonsense!' Gopu said. He picked up his bag and, thrusting his hand into the inner pocket of a tight buttoned-up grey coat (which Nagaraj had known him to possess for years), fished out an eight-anna coin to pay the fare. The jutka driver did not close his fingers on the coin but kept staring at Gopu accusingly. 'That's all. Go,' thundered Gopu. 'The avarice of these fellows has no limit.'

'Grass sells at ten annas a bundle. How can I feed the horse and myself?'

'Go away, I don't care,' cried Gopu. 'These fellows in Malgudi are spoilt by outsiders. Go, you won't get a paisa more,' whereupon Nagaraj took out of a fold at his waist in his dhoti four annas and counted it out on the man's outstretched palm. Glaring at the brothers without speaking, the driver declared the general meanness of Kabir Street dwellers, whipped his horse

and moved off. Gopu said, 'You are spoiling these
fellows. Why did you pay, as if I couldn't afford it? I
want to teach these blackguards in Malgudi a lesson.'

'Life is too short for teaching lessons—'

'You and your philosophy,' sneered Gopu, and
asked, 'Where is Tim?'

'Gone out,' said Nagaraj, somewhat nervously.

'It's six-thirty! And he is not home yet!' cried Gopu
acidly.

'Come in first, have a wash and eat something, and
then I will tell you. Come in first. Plenty of time. What
time did you leave?'

Gopu ignored the question and said, 'I'm going
back in the morning and he must come with me.'

'Where is the hurry?' Nagaraj asked apprehensively.

'He is my son and has to be with me, that's all. I'm
not bound to explain. I've tolerated his ways too long,'
he said, raising his voice.

'I'm thinking of admitting him at Albert Mission . . .'

'What for? Did you have the sense to ask me first?'

Nagaraj had no reply to this, a part of his mind
admiring his wife's cautioning him. She had said, when
Nagaraj spoke of it, 'Don't rush without consulting
your brother about Tim's studies. He may not like you
to take all that upon yourself.'

And Nagaraj had tried to silence her with, 'You
always think negatively. I know what to do with Tim.'

And she went away with a toss of her head, saying, 'Surely you know your brother—after all, aren't you brothers?'

'She has uncanny forethought,' he said to himself now. 'I should hereafter leave everything to her—all management and decisions.'

'What are you muttering to yourself, while you have nothing to say to me, and stand there blinking and mumbling like a schoolboy?' sneered Gopu.

Nagaraj realized he could not very well confess that he was secretly admiring Sita's wisdom. 'Come in. Sita will be back from the temple soon. Evenings she visits the temple.'

'Are you trying to divert my thoughts? Tell me first, where is Tim?'

They were both standing on the doorstep. The ex-engineer living in the last house was tottering back from the bar at the market. He halted in front of the house and said, 'Where is my wife? I'm wifeless but not yet a widower, sir. Pity me and yield her if you have kept her here.'

Gopu said, 'Oh, this fellow is still going strong! Let's go in.' He turned and went in. Nagaraj led the way, and first took him to Tim's room, flinging the door open. 'You remember we used to be here. Now Tim is in this room.'

'Where is Mother? How is she?' asked Gopu.

Nagaraj led him to their mother's room in the second courtyard. He whispered, 'These days she retires before sunset and wakes up before midnight and keeps calling everybody, thinking it is morning.' Gopu stood on the threshold of her darkened room and, finding her asleep, withdrew, saying, 'I will see her later before I leave.'

Sita had meanwhile returned from the temple quietly, without a sound, as a courtesy to her husband's elder brother. Gopu sat in his chair while Nagaraj kept standing. She stood in the doorway and asked, 'Shall I make coffee? Give me five minutes. I was delayed as there was a Friday crowd with their offerings.'

'I had coffee on the way at the canteen in the bus stand.'

'If I had known you were coming—a postcard would have been enough . . .' She was acting the part of junior sister-in-law (younger brother's wife) perfectly. Gopu appreciated it. Whatever might be his attitude to his brother, he was always gentle with Sita. After the formal welcome she withdrew to prepare a dinner befitting the visitor. Before going she somehow managed to signal to her husband and he quietly got up and followed her. In the hall she whispered, 'What shall I make? Should you not have warned me? How can I manage if you sit back as if you were a guest?'

'Be quick and do something,' he said. 'I know you

can . . .' He turned round and re-entered the room.

Meanwhile Gopu had taken off his shirt and coat and upper cloth and heaped them on the chair. He settled himself comfortably and remarked, 'So late, and Tim hasn't come yet! You let him loaf like this!'

'He goes out and comes home by himself,' Nagaraj explained.

'Where does he go? Don't you have to keep an eye?'

Nagaraj realized his inability to do such a thing and grinned awkwardly. Gopu glared at him in anger, 'You are strange, impossible. You have no idea what to do, where and when. You exist from day to day like a cow chewing the cud and staring at space . . .'

Nagaraj felt uncomfortable and laughed nervously, treating it as a joke.

Gopu said, 'Whatever may be the reason, he will have to come back with me, that's all. You should have turned him round and sent him to the village on the first day. Instead of that . . .'

Nagaraj had a sinking feeling at the prospect of Tim going away and said, 'I'll see that he comes to the village later.'

'Do you think I'm here to ask for a favour? I can handle him myself. Except these few days, I was the one to handle him. What do you know of boys? If he is growing in your shadow, he will be another Nagaraj.

We do not want another Nagaraj in the family.' And he laughed bitterly. Nagaraj was unaffected by this attack, took it all as an expression of Gopu's sense of humour and goodwill. He got up abruptly to go out of the room under the pretext of finding if dinner was ready. His brother, now settled on the easy chair in the room, said, 'Don't get up and try to escape. You have not lost that habit yet! Listen to me. You should have turned him back on the very first day. Instead of that you petted and pampered him, without even asking whether he took my permission before leaving home.'

'Yes, I asked him whether he had your—'

'What did he say?'

'I don't remember,' Nagaraj said.

'I want him with me. I'm adding so many things to our farm—I don't have to explain to you, but anyway you must understand the situation. Also his mother misses him and is crying all the time. He must share my labours and assist me, a grown-up boy must make himself useful. I'm putting up a gas plant which can function with the cattle refuse, which is in plenty with forty animals in the shed—the gas plant will give us light and fuel. My wife has eye trouble now, cooking with firewood, kerosene being scarce, and the smoke has affected her eyes. Also we could have gas lights.'

'Very interesting, but why disturb Tim? He is happy here.'

'If you have not realized why, I don't have to tell you anything more. Even this I have said is too much for a fellow like you.'

At this point they had to go and eat. Gopu ate in silence, not wishing to exhibit his irritation before Sita. Sita had managed to provide betel leaves and areca nut on a silver plate for chewing after dinner. Gopu and Nagaraj sat on the bench in the hall and were chewing with the contentment that comes with good food followed by proper betel-chewing.

At ten o'clock Tim knocked on the door. Gopu rushed up to open it, gazed on Tim, and said, 'After all, you found your way home!'

Tim was called in by Sita to eat.

'Is this the hour daily when he comes?' asked Gopu, and added in an undertone, 'You should spank him.'

'No, no,' Nagaraj said, shocked, and added rather idiotically, 'See how tall he has grown!' while his mind clamoured to clear the point as to what made him call Tim 'donkey'.

Tim remained silent while his father was telling him to pack up. Nagaraj felt unequal to the situation. He was afraid that Gopu might assault his son or call him 'donkey' again. If he repeated that awful explosive term, God knew what would happen. He feared that the boy might hit back in some terrible manner. He wished he could don his ochre robe and retreat into the puja room, dead for the hour, away from all strife. 'Why don't you get ready? We leave early in the morning,' shouted Gopu.

All that the boy said was, 'No, I'm staying here. I may come there for a few days, later, but now I want to be here. I am not coming home.'

Gopu let out a sigh of despair, unable to do anything else. Nagaraj felt happy to see Gopu, who always had the last word, now helpless. His aggressiveness, conceit and sharp tongue were gone. Nagaraj felt like crying out to Tim, 'Well done, my boy!' but remained silent, looking appropriately solemn. Gopu tried to change his tone. Tried persuasion. Mentioned his mother and her crying. It was also hard for Nagaraj to imagine Charu crying, she who had been so imperious and self-assured as the senior daughter-in-law of the family years ago. Nothing moved Tim. He was adamant. He just kept saying, 'I'll come later and see Mother. I want to be here.'

Next morning Gopu left in a rage, without saying goodbye, carrying his bag and walking off to find a jutka at the market corner, Nagaraj following him meekly. Gopu said, 'You go back. You have spoilt him beyond repair: you are Narada, mischief-maker. If he doesn't want to see me, I don't want to see his face either,' and went down the street briskly as Nagaraj turned back home.

Nagaraj was happy that Gopu had called him Narada abusively. He took it as a compliment. 'Narada created strife, no doubt, by passing disturbing gossip from one quarter to another, but it always proved beneficial in the long run, in an eternal perspective. Must write about him from this angle. Must write in English, of course, so that the book is widely read and people understand the concept of Narada. Must start writing on a good day like Vijaya Dasami, the day of the goddess of learning. But I'm not a writer, must be helped by someone in the line. Must consult the Talkative Man, if I can stop him for a moment when he emerges from his home while starting on his rounds. Or Professor Lingham of Albert Mission School.'

Returning, he didn't enter the house but sat on the pyol to contemplate further on Narada. The problem was that there was no authoritative source. Narada's birth was controversial. He would take him as one that just happened to be, that was all and that was sufficient. All that mattered was that he was a unique personality, the god of music. He was ever-cheerful and active, always with a song on his lips, and moved with ease among gods and demons. Blessed with extreme mobility, he traversed at a thought the skies and space, through galaxies and the Milky Way, and was welcome in all the fourteen worlds above and below this world. Gods and demons alike were friendly to him, although he was a bearer of gossip from one world to another and created strife. 'Wait till I write my book,' he addressed his brother mentally, sending his thoughts to the bus stand.

*

Going back to the past, Sita's association with Tim had begun on that day her sister-in-law brought him from her parents' home as a three-month-old baby. She took charge of him and showered on him all the maternal love bottled up within her, being childless. She bathed the child, changed his clothes and nursed him, leaving Charu free to attend to her husband's needs, embroider or read magazines by the light in the back courtyard. Her mother-in-law never ordered her or commented on her activities, as she felt slightly awed in her presence and also grateful to her for bearing a child, unlike Sita.

Various measures to cure barrenness had been suggested to Sita by her mother-in-law, who fancied herself an expert, having inherited medical knowledge from her herbalist grandfather. She would sit before Sita in the veranda of the third courtyard to supervise her chewing of neem leaves every morning, and at that time would also regale her with reminiscences.

'I remember how double-bullock carts arrived to

fetch my grandfather to distant corners of the country. He must have cured thousands of cases of barrenness, and I used to enjoy the day-long rides with Grandfather. I can still hear the jingling of the bells around the necks of trotting bullocks. He would not ride in anything less than a double-bullock carriage with proper cushions. If anyone sent an ordinary bullock-cart with a straw-covered seat, he would not come out of his room but ask me or my sister to send away the caller. And many women remained barren thereafter, for he was a determined soul. Once he said "No", it remained "No", even if the heavens pleased.'

At some stage, Sita refused to eat any more neem leaves, declaring that she preferred to remain childless. Mother-in-law said, 'Very well. Remember that there is no deficiency on our side. Nagaraj is normal. Don't you see Gopu's wife bearing a son within two years? As the proverb goes, what can the hand that holds the plough achieve, if the hand that lifts the rice pot is unlucky?' Sita bore these taunts patiently. She had given up finally after trying other remedies, such as a forty-day penance and special pujas and then pilgrimages to remote temples. Nagaraj accepted all these suggestions sheepishly. 'If we do all that Mother suggests and yet fail to breed, nobody can blame us. We will have done our best,' he would whisper to her during their bus journey to a temple sixty miles away where the carved image of a cobra was the presiding deity and had to be anointed with milk and honey from time to time, since an astrologer had analysed from the horoscope that Sita's barrenness was due to a curse on her family, an ancestor having killed a King Cobra . . .

When Tim was five years old, Nagaraj had proposed rather timidly to his brother that he put him in school. Nagaraj feared at first that his brother might turn around and say, 'What business have you to put my son to school?' but he sounded unexpectedly mild and was not averse to the proposal. Nagaraj remarked to himself, 'I do not know how to judge Gopu. He flares up unexpectedly and also listens to reason unexpectedly as he does now—strange fellow!' Gopu just said, 'Is he not too young for school?'

'Oh, no! Stephen's takes in children of three years also, very good nursery and kindergarten. Tim can enjoy the company of other children. Lots of games and playthings.'

They summoned their family priest to fix an auspicious day. Mother wanted a piper and a drummer to take the boy to school in a procession after a ceremonial inauguration at home. But it was ruled out, as Stephen's was a Mission School and they might refuse admission to a child arriving in a noisy procession. So they had to be satisfied with performing the inauguration rites at home and then conducting the boy to school dressed properly, rubbing off the sandal-paste caste mark on his forehead. 'St Stephen's is no ordinary school. It was established over a century ago; its students became judges and council members and civil servants all over the country; even in England old students of St Stephen's are found . . .' Nagaraj let his imagination wax, and his brother and mother and others listened to him with interest.

Nagaraj felt victorious on the first day Tim went to school, and escorting him back and forth became his chief occupation. He accompanied Tim while he ambled down to Stephen's, stopping to watch every little object, every crow and street puppy and sparrow on the way, dawdling along. Nagaraj indulged him to the fullest, sharing his joy and wonder. They usually arrived late at the school gate—the sister in charge was tolerant towards the nursery classes. The same process was repeated when Tim was let off at four in the afternoon, once again enjoying the spectacles on the roadside. Sometimes he spotted a donkey beside a wall and let out a whoop of astonishment and stood still gazing on it. Nagaraj also stood in wonderment, and when it threatened to prolong itself, gently pushed and piloted the youngster onward, enjoying fully every moment with Tim and through Tim.

*

Now Tim's coming promised to make life richer in the Kabir Street home. For his comfort, Nagaraj cleared the front room, furnished it with a table and chair, brought in a camp cot from the loft (which his brother had not noticed in the partitioning of properties). 'Boys must have beds and desks if they are to develop properly, unlike us, who read our lessons in any corner and slept in corridors, if not in cattle sheds. Our parents were indifferent. That's the reason why I am like this . . .' He paused to question his own statement. 'Like what? Nothing wrong with us. Gopu was a first class BA. He has his defects but was a studious fellow—but he always had his room and table: I was the one shunted out hither and thither and had to do my homework in any corner available. No wonder I failed in BA and scraped through a third class later . . .'

After this recollection his thoughts returned to Tim's needs. He told Tim, 'Here is your room, you may shut yourself in and sit at your desk, read, read and read all day, and nobody will disturb you . . .' Next, he took Tim to Albert Mission Junior College, saw his friend Jesudoss, the headmaster, and got him admitted, explaining, 'His early years were at Stephen's but his father moved to the village and his studies were interrupted . . .'

Nagaraj's mind was seething with plans for his

nephew. Must consult Rajan of Rajan Cycle Mart about a bicycle for Tim and then must take him to Bari, the loquacious stationer, in order to pile on his desk paper and notebooks, and then to watch the young man in his room bent over his studies—a vision which stirred him deeply. This was an ideal place for study, absolutely silent and quiet but for his old mother's constant movement over the whole place. If the door was shut she was bound to knock on it to ask why, and not rest till it was opened. But this was a minor problem. Tim should not mind it. He was fond of his grandmother and was seen now and then sitting on her bed chatting. If he just opened the door and said he was at his studies, she was bound to feel pleased and leave him alone.

The old mother, however, did not live long enough to enjoy her grandson's company. In less than three months after his arrival she was gone. She tumbled down during her perambulation through the vast acreage of the house and was bedridden, with Tim nursing her, without leaving her side even for a moment. To cremate her, Gopu, as the elder son, came down with his family, performed the funeral rites correctly and left in a businesslike manner on the fourteenth day, hardly exchanging half-a-dozen words with Tim. His mother, Charu, made constant but infructuous attempts to persuade him to return home.

ON THE SANDS OF
THE SARAYU

[Chandran, a collegegoer in the novel The Bachelor
of Arts, *spots a girl named Malathi on the banks of
the river Sarayu—and falls head over heels in love.
The following excerpt is a delightful account of the
first stirrings of love.]*

IT WAS ON one of his river ramblings that Chandran
met Malathi and thought that he would not have room
for anything else in his mind. No one can explain the
attraction between two human beings. It happens.

One evening he came to the river, and was loafing
along it, when he saw a girl, about fifteen years old,
playing with her younger sister on the sand. Chandran
had been in the habit of staring at every girl who sat
on the sand, but he had never felt before the acute
interest he felt in this girl now. He liked the way she
sat; he liked the way she played with her sister; he

liked the way she dug her hands into the sand and threw it in the air. He paused only for a moment to observe the girl. He would have willingly settled there and spent the rest of his life watching her dig her hands into the sand. But that could not be done. There were a lot of people about.

He passed on. He went forward a few paces and wanted to turn back and take another look at the girl. But that could not be done. He felt that the scores of persons squatting on the sand were all watching him.

He went on his usual walk down to Nallappa's Grove, crossed the river, went up the opposite bank, and away into the fields there; but he caught himself more than once thinking of the girl. How old was she? Probably fourteen. Might be even fifteen or sixteen. If she was more than fourteen she must be married. There was a touch of despair in this thought. What was the use of thinking of a married girl? It would be very improper. He tried to force his mind to think of other things. He tried to engage it in his favourite subject—his trip to England in the coming year. If he was going to England how was he to dress himself? He had better get used to ties and shoes and coats and hats and knives and forks. He would get a first-class degree in England and come back and marry. What was the use of thinking of a married girl? Probably she was not married. Her parents were very likely to be rational and modern, people who abhorred the custom of rushing a young child into marriage. He tried to analyse why he was thinking of her. Why did he think of her so much? Was it her looks? Was she so good-looking as all that? Who could say? He hadn't noticed her before. Then how could he say that she was the most beautiful girl in the world? When did he say that? Didn't he? If not, why was he thinking of her so much? Chandran was puzzled, greatly puzzled by the whole thing.

He wondered next what her name might be. She looked like one with the name of Lakshmi. Quite a beautiful name, the name of the goddess of wealth, the spouse of the god Vishnu, who was the protector of creatures.

That night he went home very preoccupied. It was at five o'clock that he had seen her, and at nine he was still thinking of her.

After dinner he did not squat on the carpet in the hall, but preferred to go to his room and remain there alone. He tried to read a little; he was in the middle of Wells's *Tono Bungay*. He had found the book gripping, but now he felt it was obtrusive. He was irritated. He put away the book and sat staring at the wall. He presently realized that darkness would be more soothing. He blew out the lamp and sat in his chair. Suppose, though unmarried, she belonged to some other caste? A marriage would not be tolerated even between sub-sects of the same caste. If India was to attain salvation these watertight divisions must go—community, caste, sects, sub-sects, and still further divisions. He felt very indignant. He would set an example himself by marrying this girl whatever her caste or sect might be.

The next day he shaved with great care and paid a great deal of attention to his hair, and awaited the evening. When evening came he put on his chocolate-coloured tweed coat and started out. At five he was on the river bank, squatting on the sand near the spot where he had seen the girl the previous day. He sat there for over two hours. The girl did not come. Dozens of other townspeople came to the river and sprawled all over the place, but not that girl. Chandran rose and walked along, peering furtively at every group. It was a very keen search, but it brought forth nothing. Why wasn't she there? His heart beat fast at the sight of every figure that approached the river clad in a saree. It was seven-forty-five when he set his face homeward, feeling that his brilliantine, shave, ironed tweed coat were all wasted.

The next day he again went to the river and again waited till seven-forty-five in the evening, and went home dispirited. He tossed in bed all night. In moments he whispered the word 'Lakshmi', 'Lakshmi'. He suddenly pulled himself up and laughed at himself: it looked as if the girl had paid a first and last visit to the river, and it seemed more than likely that she belonged to another caste, and was married. What a fool he was to go on thinking of her night and day for three whole days. It was a ridiculous obsession. His sobriety ought to assert itself now. An idle brain was the devil's workshop. Too true. A brain given rest for over nine months brought one to this state.

He rose in the morning with a haggard face. His mother asked him if he was not well. Chandran felt that some explanation was due and said he had a terrible headache. His mother, standing two inches shorter than him, put out her hands, stroked his temples, gave him special coffee, and advised him to stay at home the whole day. Chandran felt that nothing could be better than that. He decided not to shave or comb his hair or wear a coat and go out. For he feared that if he went out he might be tempted to go on the foolish quest.

He stayed in his room all day. His father came in at midday and kept him company. He sat in the chair and talked of this and that. Chandran realized all of a sudden that he had better leave Malgudi. That would solve the problem.

'Father, will you let me go to Madras?'

'By all means, if you'd like a change.'

'I suppose it will be very hot there?'

'Must be. The saying is that Madras is hot for ten months in the year and hotter for two.'

'Then I don't want to go and fry myself there,' said Chandran.

'Try some other place. You can go to your aunt at Bangalore.'

'No, no. She will keep telling me what jewels she has got for her daughter. I can't stand her.' He decided that he would stay in the best place on earth, home.

Mother came in at about three o'clock to ask how he was feeling. His brother came in at four-thirty, as soon as school was over, and stood near Chandran's bed, staring at him silently.

'What is it?' Chandran asked.

'Nothing. Why are you in bed?'

'Never mind why. What is the news in the school?'

'We are playing against the YMU on Saturday. After that we are meeting the Board School Eleven. What we can't understand is why the captain has left out Mohideen. He is bound to have a lot of trouble over that. People are prepared to take it up to the headmaster.'

Chandran could not stay in bed beyond six-thirty. He got up, opened all the windows, washed his face, combed his hair, put on a coat (not the tweed one), and went out. What he needed, he told himself, was plenty of fresh air and exercise and things to think about. Since he wanted exercise he decided to avoid the riverside. The place, he persuaded himself, was stale and crowded. He wished today to take a walk at the very opposite end of the town, the Trunk Road. He walked a mile along the Trunk Road and turned back. He hurried back across Lawley Extension, Market Road and the North Street, and reached the river. It was dark and most people had gone home.

Chandran saw her again at the river bank next evening. She was wearing a green saree, and playing with her little companion. Chandran saw her from a distance and went towards her as if drawn by a rope. But, on approaching her, his courage failed him, and he walked away in the opposite direction. Presently he stopped and blamed himself for wasting a good opportunity of making his person familiar to her; he turned once again with the intention of passing before her closely, slowly, and deliberately. At a distance he could look at her, but when he came close he felt self-conscious and awkward, and while passing actually in front of her he bent his head, fixed his gaze on the ground, and walked fast. He was away, many yards away, from her in a moment. He checked his pace once again and looked back for a fraction of a second, and was quite thrilled at the sight of the green saree in the distance. He did not dare to look longer; for he was obsessed with the feeling that he was being observed by the whole crowd on the river bank ... He hoped that she had observed him. He hoped that she had noted his ironed coat. He stood there and debated with himself whether she had seen him or not. One part of him said that she could not have observed him, because he had walked very fast and because there were a lot of people passing and repassing on the sand. Chandran steadily discouraged this sceptical half of his mind, and lent his wholehearted support to the other half, which was saying that just as he had noticed her in a crowd she was sure to have noticed him. Destiny always worked that way. His well-ironed chocolate tweed was sure to invite notice. He hoped that he didn't walk clumsily in front of her. He again told himself she must have noticed that he was not like the rest of the crowd. And so why should he not now go and occupy a place that would be close to her and in the direct line of her vision? Starting was half the victory in love. His sceptical half now said that by this procedure he might scare her off the river for ever; but, said the other half, tomorrow she may not come to the river at all, and if you don't start an eye friendship immediately, you may not get the opportunity again for a million years ... He was engaged in this internal controversy when he received a slap on the back and saw Veeraswami and Mohan, his old classmates, behind him.

'How are you, Chandran? It seems years since we met.'

'We met only last March, less than a year, you know,' said Chandran.

Mohan asked: 'Chandran, do you remember the evening we spent in your room, reading poetry?'

'Yes, yes. What have you done with your poems?'

'They are still with me.'

Chandran felt all his courtesy exhausted. He was not keen on reunions just then. He tried to get away. But Veeraswami would not let him go: 'A year since we met. I have been dying to see an old classmate, and you want to cut me! Won't you come and have a little coffee with us in some restaurant?' He hooked his arm in Chandran's and dragged him along. Chandran tried to resist, and then said: 'Let us go this way. I promised to meet somebody. I must see if he is there . . .' He pointed down the river, past the spot of green saree. They went in that direction. Mohan inquired three times what Chandran was doing and received no reply; Veeraswami was talking without a pause. Chandran pretended to listen to him, but constantly turned his head to his left and stole glances at something there; he had to do this without being noticed by his friends. Finally, when he passed before her, he looked at her for so short a space of time that she appeared only as a passing green blur . . . Before leaving the river bank he looked back only twice. He heartily disliked his companions.

'What are you doing now, Chandran?' Mohan asked, undefeated.

'Nothing at present. I am going to England in a few months.'

At this Veeraswami started a heated discourse on the value of going to England. 'What have we to learn from the English? I don't know when this craze for going to England will stop. It is a drain on the country's resources. What have we to learn from the English?'

'I may be going there to teach them something,' said Chandran. Even granted that she had not noticed him the first time, she couldn't have helped noticing him when he passed before her again; that was why he didn't look at her fully; he didn't want to embarrass her by meeting her gaze.

'Shall we go to the Welcome?' Veeraswami asked.

They had now left the river and were in North Street.

'Anywhere,' Chandran said mechanically.

'You seem to be worried over something,' Veeraswami said.

'Oh, nothing. I am sorry.' Chandran pulled himself up resolutely. Here were two fellows eager for his company, and he had no business to be absorbed in distant thoughts.

'Forgive me,' he said again.

They were now before the Welcome Restaurant, a small, smoky building, from which the smell of sweets and burning ghee assailed the nostrils of passers-by in the street.

They sat round an oily table in the dark hall. Serving boys were shouting menus and bills and were dashing hither and thither. A server came and asked: 'What will you have, sir?'

'What shall we have?'

'What will you have?'

'I want only coffee.'

'Have something with it.'

'Impossible. Only coffee.'

'Bring three cups of coffee, good, strong.'

Chandran asked: 'What are you doing, Mohan? Did you get through?'

'No. I failed, and my uncle cut off my allowance. I am now the Malgudi correspondent of the *Daily Messenger* of Madras. They have given me the whole district. They pay me three-eight per column of twenty-one inches.'

'Are you making much money?'

'Sometimes fifty, sometimes ten. It all depends on those rascals, mad fellows. Sometimes they cut everything that I send.'

'It is a moderate paper,' Veeraswami said jeeringly.

'I am not concerned with their policy,' Mohan said.

'What are you doing?' Chandran asked, turning to Veeraswami.

'It will take a whole day for me to tell you. I am starting a movement called the Resurrection Brigade. I am touring about a lot on that business.'

'What is the brigade?'

'It is only an attempt to prepare the country for revolution. Montagu-Chelmsford reforms, Simon Report, and what not, are all a fraud. Our politicians, including the Congressmen, are playing into the hands of the Imperialists. The Civil Disobedience Movement is a childish business. Our brigade will gain the salvation of our country by an original method. Will you join it? Mohan is already a member.'

Chandran promised to think it over, and asked what they expected Mohan to do for the movement.

'Everything. We want everybody there, poets, philosophers, musicians, sculptors, and swordsmen.'

'What is its strength now?'

'About twenty-five have so far signed the brigade pledge. I expect that in two years we shall have a membership of 50,000 in south India alone.'

They finished their coffee and rose. They went back to the river, smoked cigarettes, and talked all the evening. Before parting, Chandran promised to see them again and asked them where they lived.

'I am staying with Mohan,' said Veeraswami.

'Where do you live, Mohan?'

'Room 14, Modern Indian Lodge, Mill Street.'

'Right. I shall drop in sometime,' said Chandran.

'I won't be in town after Tuesday. I am going into the country for six months,' said Veeraswami.

Chandran realized that friends and acquaintances were likely to prove a nuisance to him by the river. He decided to cut everyone hereafter. With this resolution he went to the Sarayu bank next evening. He also decided to be very bold, and indifferent to the public's observation and criticism.

She was there with her little companion.

Chandran went straight to a spot just thirty yards from where she sat, and settled down there. He had determined to stare at her this evening. He might even throw in an elegant wink or smile. He was going to stare at her and take in a lot of details regarding her features. He had not made out yet whether she was fair or light brown; whether she had long hair or short, and whether her eyes were round or almond-shaped; and he had also some doubts about her nose.

He sat at this thirty-yards range and kept throwing at her a side glance every fifth second. He noticed that she played a great deal with her little companion. He wanted to go to her and ask whether the little companion was her sister or cousin and how old she was. But he abandoned the idea. A man of twenty-two going up and conversing with a grown-up girl, a perfect stranger, would be affording a very uncommon sight to the public.

This optical communion became a daily habit. His powers of observation and deduction increased tremendously. He gathered several facts about the girl. She wore a dark saree and a green saree alternatively. She came to the river chiefly for the sake of her little companion. She was invariably absent on Fridays and came late on Wednesdays. Chandran concluded from this that the girl went to the temple on Friday evenings, and was delayed by a music master or a stitching master on Wednesdays. He further gathered that she was of a religious disposition, and was accomplished in the art of music or embroidery. From her regularity he concluded that she was a person of very systematic habits. The fact that she played with her young companion showed that she had a loving disposition. He concluded that she had no brothers, since not a single soul escorted her on any evening. Encouraged by this conclusion, he wondered if he should not stop her and talk to her when she rose to go home. He might even accompany her to her house. That might become a beautiful habit. What wonderful things he would have to say to her. When the traffic of the town had died, they could walk together under the moon or in magic starlight. He would stop a few yards from her house. What a parting of sweetness and pain! . . . It must be noted that in this dream the young companion did not exist, or, if she did, she came to the river and went home all by herself.

An evening of this optical fulfilment filled him with tranquillity. He left the river and went home late in the evening, meditating on God, and praying to Him with concentration that He would bless this romance with success. All night he repeated her name, 'Lakshmi', and fervently hoped that her soul heard his call through the night.

He had lived for over a month in a state of bliss, notwithstanding his ignorance. He began to feel now that he ought to be up and doing and get a little more practical. He could not go on staring at her on the sands all his life. He must know all about her.

He followed her at a distance of about half a furlong on a dark evening when she returned home from the river. He saw her enter a house in Mill Street. He paced before the house slowly, twice, slowing up to see if there was any board before the house. There was none.

He remembered suddenly that Mohan lived in Mill Street. Room number 14, Modern Indian Lodge, he had said. He went up and down the street in search of the hotel. At last he found that it was the building opposite the girl's house. There was a signboard, but that could not be seen in the dark. Room number 14 was half a cubicle on the staircase landing. The cubicle was divided by a high wooden partition into Room 14 and Room 15.

Mohan was delighted to receive Chandran.

'Has Veeraswami gone?' Chandran asked.

'Weeks ago,' replied Mohan.

There was not a single table or chair in the room. Mohan slept on a striped carpet spread on the floor. He sat on it reclining against the wooden partition. There was a yellow trunk in a corner of the room, on which a shining nickel flower-vase was kept with some paper flowers in it. The room received its light and ventilation from the single window in Room 15, over the wooden partition. A bright gas lamp hung over the wooden partition and shed its greenish glare impartially on Room 14 and Room 15.

'Would you believe it? I have never been in this street before,' said Chandran.

'Indeed! But why should you come here? You live at the south end while this is the east end of the town.'

'I like this street,' Chandran said. 'I wonder why this is called Mill Street. Are all the people that live here mill-owners?'

'Nothing of the kind. Years ago there were two weaving mills at the end of the street. There are all sorts of people here.'

'Oh. Any particularly important person?'

'None that I can think of.'

It was on Chandran's lips, at this point, to ask who lived in the opposite house. But he merely said that he wished to meet his friend oftener in his room.

'I go out news-hunting at ten in the morning and return at about four, after posting my letters. I do not usually go out after that. You can come any time you please,' said Mohan.

'Have you no holidays?'

'On Sundays we have no paper. And so on Saturday I have a holiday. I spend the whole day in the room. Please do come any time you like, and as often as you like.'

'Thanks, thanks. I have absolutely no company. I shall be delighted to come here frequently.'